ROYAL RANSOM

Hattie Beaumont cleared her throat. "There are several other things we need to talk about," she said. "The matter, for one, of Winterset's ownership."

"The mare that was stolen doesn't belong to you, then?"

"That's correct," Hattie Beaumont said. "She boards here."

"Does it make any difference who owns her?"

"Ordinarily," Hattie Beaumont said, "I would say it wouldn't. But this is a slightly different situation. You see, Winterset belongs to the Queen of England."

Other Avon Books by
John Birkett

THE LAST PRIVATE EYE

Avon Books are available at special quantity discounts for bulk purchases for sales promotions, premiums, fund raising or educational use. Special books, or book excerpts, can also be created to fit specific needs.

For details write or telephone the office of the Director of Special Markets, Avon Books, Dept. FP, 105 Madison Avenue, New York, New York 10016, 212-481-5653.

THE QUEEN'S MARE

JOHN BIRKETT

AVON BOOKS • NEW YORK

This one is for Birketts and their families:
The Kid
Julie, Ellen, Lynn
Patrick, Mary Kathleen, Larry, and Mick
And in memory of Blackie and Frances
And with great appreciation and thanks to Betty Receiver

THE QUEEN'S MARE is an original publication of Avon Books. This work has never before appeared in book form. This work is a novel. Any similarity to actual persons or events is purely coincidental.

AVON BOOKS
A division of
The Hearst Corporation
105 Madison Avenue
New York, New York 10016

Copyright © 1990 by John Birkett
Published by arrangement with the author
ISBN: 0-380-75683-8

All rights reserved, which includes the right to reproduce this book or portions thereof in any form whatsoever except as provided by the U.S. Copyright Law. For information address Jane Rotrosen Agency, 318 East 51st Street, New York, New York 10022.

First Avon Books Printing: July 1990

AVON TRADEMARK REG. U.S. PAT. OFF. AND IN OTHER COUNTRIES, MARCA REGISTRADA, HECHO EN U.S.A.

Printed in the U.S.A.

RA   10 9 8 7 6 5 4 3 2 1

ONE

It was a Monday morning in May, a couple of weeks after the Derby, and I was sitting in my office with my feet propped up on the desk looking through the *Racing Form*. The Derby had been won by a longshot who'd paid 37 dollars and 40 cents. My pick was still running.

When the telephone rang. McGraw was seated at her desk, filing her fingernails. She made no move to answer the phone. I was two weeks behind on her salary, and this was her way of retaliating. I put down the *Form* and picked up my extension.

"Rhineheart Investigations."

"May I speak to Mr. Rhineheart, please?" The speaker on the other end of the line had an old woman's voice, thin, querulous, well spoken.

"This is him," I said.

McGraw's upper lip curled into a sneer. "*He*," she said loudly. "'*This is he*' is the correct way to say that."

"Mr. Rhineheart. My name is Hattie Beaumont. I am interested in exploring the possibility of obtaining your services. I wonder if we could possibly meet this afternoon."

Hattie Beaumont. The caption under her photographs in the newspaper usually read *The Grand Dame of Kentucky Racing*. She owned Ashtree Farms, which was just outside of Louisville and was one of the largest Thoroughbred breeding farms in Kentucky. Ashtree had bred several Kentucky Derby winners, and the sires

1

and dams of a dozen more. It had an international reputation, as did its owner. Getting a phone call from Hattie Beaumont was something of a surprise. It was on the order of getting a call from the Governor of the Commonwealth, or someone like that.

"You sure you got the right Rhineheart?" I asked. "My name's Michael. I'm a private eye."

"I know exactly who you are, Mr. Rhineheart. How does two o'clock this afternoon suit you?"

"That's fine," I said.

"Do you know the way to Ashtree?" she asked.

"I'll find it," I said. "And I'll see you at two, Mrs. Beaumont."

When she heard the name *Beaumont* McGraw sat up straight and shot a questioning look in my direction.

I put down the phone, and with a blank look on my face picked up the *Form* and pretended to read it.

McGraw jumped up, dashed over, and snatched the *Form* out of my hand.

"*Who* was that on the phone?" she demanded.

"If you'd answered it," I said, "like you're supposed to, then you'd know, wouldn't you?"

She doubled up her little fist—McGraw is four-foot-eleven and ninety pounds—and gave me a shot in the bicep.

"Come on, Rhineheart. Who was it? It wasn't *the* Mrs. Beaumont, was it?"

I nodded.

"Bullshit," McGraw said.

"Have it your own way," I said. "But put it down in the appointment book that I'm going to meet with Hattie Beaumont at her place at two clock."

"This afternoon?"

I nodded.

"At Ashtree Farms?"

"Two for two, McGraw."

"Out in Prospect?"

"Right again."

"Take me with you," she said.

"Get serious," I said.

"Please."

"Don't be silly," I said. "Why would I want to haul you along?"

"It'd be good training," McGraw said.

"For who?"

"That's *whom*," McGraw said. A perpetual student who took every half-ass course the local colleges had to offer, she was suffering from one too many night-school sessions in English grammar. Lately, every time I opened my mouth, McGraw could be counted on to correct my usage. "Not 'for who.' 'For whom' is the correct way to say that. Objective case. Whom is the—"

"Stuff it, McGraw."

"—object of for," she plunged on, without missing a beat, then added, "Good training for *me* is what I meant. Some actual on-the-job detective training, instead of research and typing and answering the phone."

"Which you don't do anyway," I said. "I'm the one who answered the goddamn phone." I was getting as illogical as McGraw, whose big dream in life was to become a private eye. I had mixed feelings about the whole thing. If she ever achieved her goal, I would lose, it was true, a rotten secretary, one who couldn't even answer the phone properly, let alone type and file. On the other hand, it was entirely possible that if she worked for me as an operative she would be an even worse investigator. Any way you looked at it, I came out on the losing end.

"Say I took you out there," I said. "What reason would I give Mrs. Beaumont for bringing along my secretary?"

"You could introduce me as your associate," McGraw said.

"Forget it." I stood up and smoothed out the lapels of my sport coat. "Do I look all right?"

McGraw got up on her tiptoes to straighten my collar. "You look like you always look. Your clothes are one big wrinkle." She gave the general area of my left shoulder a bad look.

"What's wrong with you?"

"You're packing, aren't you?" She was talking about my Colt Python, which was stuck in a shoulder holster under my arm.

"Yeah."

"You're not going to wear it out to Ashtree, are you?"

"Is that bad form, or something?"

"It's the pits of tackiness."

"That's me, babe." I headed for the door.

"I'll be here when you get back," McGraw said.

TWO

There was a main entrance with a guardhouse and two heavily armed security guards manning it. They wore the uniforms of a well-known national investigative agency. I had to show my I.D. to one guard who scrutinized it thoroughly while the other one phoned up to the main house. They let me through finally and I gunned my car—a '76 Maverick on its last legs—up the paved driveway which looked long enough and wide enough to accommodate light aircraft.

The house at the other end of the driveway was huge, a couple of stories tall, and old. It dated back to the turn of the century. It was built out of red brick that had weathered and lightened over the decades into a pale roselike patina. I parked the car between a silver Mercedes and a two-tone gray and black van with white-walled tires and mud flaps. Silver lettering on the van door read Ashtree Farms, Prospect, Kentucky. I trudged along a walk and climbed up a set of stone steps to a porch that was big enough to park a tank on.

The front door, which was made of thick dark cherry wood, was flanked on each side by narrow, leaded windows. Above the door was a fan window. There was a brass nameplate that read Main House—Ashtree Farms. There was a doorbell and a burnished brass knocker. You had your choice. I pressed the bell.

The door was opened after a minute by a beautiful girl with large brown eyes, a sweet youthful face, and a mass of thick dark hair that curled across her shoulders. She was wearing a V-neck sweater that was all V and a denim miniskirt. Somehow, anklet sox and a pair of beat-up Reebok's made the long, fine-looking legs that flowed down from under the short skirt seem even longer and finer. She had thick dark lashes and a wide mouth and when she smiled a wicked, sexy smile at me my heart paused a moment, then picked up its erratic beat, and my own lips drew back involuntarily. I stood there with a goofy smile on my face and said nothing until she spoke.

"Can I help you?"

I cleared my throat, told myself to be cool—she was just a coed, a college kid—and put a sober, businesslike look on my face.

"My name's Rhineheart," I said.

"Are you the private investigator?" she asked and there was, I noted, a trace of awe—either fake or real, I couldn't tell—in her voice.

I nodded.

"I'm Paige Beaumont Cavanaugh," she hummed. Her voice was full of throaty musical tones.

"Nice to meet you, Paige."

"Please come in." She turned her body slightly and as I entered she leaned forward and managed to brush her breasts against my right arm. I resisted the temptation to rub the spot on my arm, which immediately began to tingle.

I stepped into a high-ceilinged, carpeted entrance hall that was furnished with antique tables and gilded mirrors.

Paige closed the front door, then led me into a room on the left. Large and imposing and lined on all sides with rows of books that ran from floor to ceiling, it was, obviously, the library. Set in the far wall was a pair of French doors that looked out on an English garden and the 6,000 or so acres of Thoroughbred horse farm that surrounded the main house.

"Grandmother will be with you in a minute," Paige said. "Can I get you anything in the meantime. A drink?" She ran her tongue across her lips. "Anything?"

I looked at her closely. Was she putting me on, jiving me? Her skin gave off a glow like it had its own source of illumination. It was impossible to guess her age. Somewhere between seventeen, I judged, and twenty-five. And trouble itself. The very thing.

"No thanks," I said.

"I call her 'Grandmother,' but actually," Paige said, "she's really my great-grandmother. She's my mother's grandmother." Paige turned her big eyes on me. "Do you know my mother, Mr. Rhineheart?"

"I don't think so," I said.

"She's a very famous actress," Paige said.

"I don't know too many actresses," I said.

"You're the first private detective I've ever met," Paige said. "I love private detective shows on TV," she said, her tone suddenly youthful and enthusiastic. "They're my absolute favorite. The detectives drive around in Maseratis and act so cool and everything."

"Uh-huh." The only Maserati I had ever seen was in a magazine photograph.

"Grandmother is going to have you find the mare, isn't she?"

"What mare is that?" I asked.

"Her name is Winterset," Paige said, "and she belongs to the—"

"Paige!"

The girl's name was uttered in a voice that managed to sound soft-spoken and authoritative at the same time. I turned and saw an old woman walking slowly across the room toward us. The woman was small and frail-looking and she moved deliberately, leaning heavily on a thick black cane. She wore a simple black linen dress and flat-heeled shoes with bows on them. Her hair was white and she wore it pulled back from her face, which was pale and lined with wrinkles. Up close, her features were sharp and distinct: a long nose, prominent cheekbones. She had bright brown eyes, the look of a hawk. In person, she didn't resemble her newspaper photographs at all.

Her grip was firm but in my hand hers felt small, bony, and cold.

"I'm Hattie Beaumont."

"Michael Rhineheart."

Hattie Beaumont turned to Paige. "Paige, dear, would you mind leaving us alone? Mr. Rhineheart and I have some business to discuss."

The girl leaned over and kissed her great-grandmother on the cheek. She curled her fingers and gave me a little schoolgirl's goodbye wave—"Nice to have met you, Mr. Rhineheart"—and hurried out of the room.

Hattie Beaumont watched her leave. "Paige," she said, "is my granddaughter Charlotte's child. Her last name is Cavanaugh, which is the name of the man Charlotte was married to. Very temporarily, I might add. Are you familiar with my granddaughter Charlotte, Mr. Rhineheart?"

"I don't think so," I said.

"Well, if you have the opportunity to meet her—and I'm sure you will—never tell her that you don't recognize her name. It will break her heart. Charlotte is an *actress*, Mr. Rhineheart, and she is under the impression that everyone in America has seen her on the stage and is familiar with her entire career."

Hattie Beaumont pointed to a large, comfortable-looking armchair. "Please sit down, Mr. Rhineheart."

I sat down, and Hattie Beaumont eased herself carefully into a high-backed rocking chair across from me.

"Tell me about your family, Mr. Rhineheart."

"My family?"

"I am a great believer in family. Are you married?"

THE QUEEN'S MARE

I thought about Catherine, my wife, who had died in an accident.

"Not anymore."

"Do you have any children, Mr. Rhineheart?"

"No."

"I had one," Hattie Beaumont said. "A son. He's dead now. He's been dead for twenty-five years. He had two daughters, my grandchildren, whom I brought up as if they were my own. Well, of course, they are my own. Charlotte, Paige's mother, and Shirley, the oldest. They are my grandchildren, but they have been raised as if they were my daughters. And the truth is Paige is more like a daughter than a great-grandchild. She lives with me. I have raised her since she was a small child. Her father never visits her. Her mother, I'm afraid, has no time for her. She is too busy with her *career*." Hattie Beaumont leaned forward suddenly, a wicked look in her eye. "How old would you guess she is, Mr. Rhineheart? I mean Paige, of course?"

I shrugged. "I have no idea."

"She turned fifteen last week."

Fifteen? That smoldering sexpot? Holy Christ! I cleared my throat. "She looks a bit older than that," I said.

Hattie Beaumont smiled.

"My operations director, Diane Carter, is going to join us in a little while," she said. "We'll have some tea, if that's all right with you, Mr. Rhineheart."

"Sure."

"Of course, we have something harder, if you prefer." Hattie Beaumont's voice was thin. She spoke slowly and softly, but if you listened closely, you could hear the flint underneath.

"Tea's fine," I said.

"Did you have a pleasant drive out here, Mr. Rhineheart?"

"Pleasant enough," I said.

"And does the weather suit you?"

The weather? What did the weather have to do with anything? Was I there for a chitchat? Were we going to have a little tea party and socialize? "The weather's fine," I said.

Hattie Beaumont settled herself in her chair. "I'm going to proceed on the assumption that you are familiar with our operation here at Ashtree. Am I correct about that, Mr. Rhineheart?"

I looked the old woman in the eye. "I know about Ashtree, and I know who you are, too, Mrs. Beaumont. Why'd you ask me here?"

She tried to hide a smile. "I heard that about you, Mr. Rhineheart. Someone told me you could be rather abrupt at times."

"Crude's probably a better word for it," I said. "Another way of looking at it," I added, "is that I don't like to waste a lot of time."

"Good," Hattie Beaumont said. "Neither do I. I asked you here to take on a piece of work for me. I've made some inquiries about you. As a private investigator you're a figure of some notoriety, but you have a reputation for being tough and for being a man who can keep a confidence." She peered over at me. "Is that the case?"

I nodded. That was pretty much the case.

"Then I'll get straight to the point," Hattie Beaumont said. "Something dreadful has happened. One of the broodmares stabled here at Ashtree has been . . . kidnapped . . . stolen. Along with her foal, a ten-day-old colt. They were taken from the foaling barn the night before last." Hattie Beaumont paused. "Yesterday evening I received a telephone call. A man . . . a man's voice . . . muffled in some way, demanding a sum of money in return for the mare and her foal."

"How much money?" I asked.

"A million dollars," Hattie Beaumont said.

THREE

A million dollars.

In different circumstances, I might have puckered up and cut loose with a whistle. It was, by anyone's standard, a formidable amount of money.

"The mare alone," Hattie Beaumont said, "is worth far more than a million dollars. So is the foal, of course. In any way that really matters, they're priceless. You understand that, don't you, Mr. Rhineheart?"

"Sure," I said, as if I knew all about priceless. *Sure?* Priceless was way the hell out of my league. When I worked, I got $250 a day. Plus expenses. Most of my clients thought that the two-fifty was too much.

"I have not talked to the police regarding this," Hattie Beaumont said.

I looked at her. "Are you telling me that the police haven't been informed about the theft?"

"They haven't been told about the theft or the ransom demand," Hattie Beaumont said.

"Why not?"

"For several reasons, Mr. Rhineheart. In addition to their obvious monetary value, the mare and the foal are very important and valuable animals in terms of their breeding and racing potential. The mare's name is Winterset. She is a daughter of Queen's Crown. Winterset's foal was sired by BuckMaster. Are you familiar with BuckMaster, Mr. Rhineheart?"

According to the last *Thoroughbred Record* I'd read,

BuckMaster was the leading money-winning sire in North America. He stood at Ashtree Farms.

I said, "Yes, I've heard of him."

"I want the mare and the foal returned safely," Hattie Beaumont said. "And I'm not convinced that telling the authorities about the theft and ransom demand will help me achieve that. I want them returned even if I have to pay the ransom to do it." She paused a moment, then went on. "Publicity is also an important consideration. This must be kept as quiet as possible. Ashtree Farms has a reputation as one of the finest breeding venues in all of racing. Mares from all over the world board here. The extent and type of publicity attached to a theft of this kind would not be in our interests."

"All that's fine," I said, "but the cops have this tendency to get upset when they're not told about everything that concerns them."

Hattie Beaumont nodded. "I'm aware of that, Mr. Rhineheart, and I'll take full responsibility for not informing them. There is another reason for keeping this confidential. It has to do with the fact that Ashtree Farms is in the midst of a battle for survival. As I am speaking to you there is a struggle among various stockholder factions for control of the farm and the racing stable. Not to put too fine a point on it, there is a move to unseat me as CEO and Chairman of the Board of Ashtree. Needless to say, I am fighting this with all the means at my disposal."

"You think the theft and this power struggle are connected?"

"I have no idea, but it would not surprise me. I do know if the news of the theft becomes public, it almost certainly will not help me, Mr. Rhineheart. So far, only a few people know about the theft and the ransom demand. Most of the employees of the farm, of course, know about the theft. They are a loyal group of people, but of course there is no way to ensure their silence. It seems to be only a matter of time before the police find out about everything. Which is why we have to work fast, Mr. Rhineheart."

"Whoa." I held up a hand. "Mrs. Beaumont, I'm not a bad detective, but I'm not the fastest operator or the quickest sleuth in the business. I just kind of plod along and bump into things. If I go to work for you, it's going to take me some time to find out who stole your mare."

Hattie Beaumont smiled. "Mr. Rhineheart, let's be clear about things. My main aim in hiring you is *not* to discover who is responsible for stealing the mare and her foal. What I am interested in having you do is act as my representative in all transactions with the thieves. I'm speaking of negotiating arrangements, protecting the ransom money, delivering it, seeing to the safe return of the mare and the foal, and so forth. I'm told that you have performed similar jobs in the past and that you have done them well."

She was referring to the role I had played in what the Louisville and Lexington papers had called the Underwood Case. The son of a prominent Fayette County horse breeder had been kidnapped. I had been brought in, and in a relatively brief period of time had arranged for the delivery of the ransom and the return of the victim. It had been luck as much as anything, and I had received some favorable if unwanted publicity.

I thought it over. In some ways it was little more than a glorified delivery boy's job, but the fact that the deal involved a couple of priceless Thoroughbreds gave it a lot more possibilities than the prospect of chasing after someone's sixteen-year-old runaway kid. There was that and there was the wrinkle of working a case that involved me in the affairs of Hattie Beaumont and Ashtree farms.

"I charge two hundred and fifty a day," I said.

"That seems quite reasonable," Hattie Beaumont said.

"Plus expenses."

"Of course."

"And I usually get an advance," I added.

"I'll see to it you have a check this afternoon." She looked toward the doorway and smiled. "Ah, here's Miss Hackett. And Diane."

I turned around to see two women enter the room. One was a thin woman with short light brown hair who was pushing a cart before her. The other was a younger blond-haired woman in a green knit dress. The cart came to a stop alongside Hattie's chair. On it, sat a silver tea service that looked like it was worth the amount of ransom money the thieves had mentioned. The dark-haired woman began to fuss with the tea things.

Hattie Beaumont said, "Stop that, Meg, and say hello to Mr. Rhineheart. He's the private detective I told you about. Mr. Rhineheart, this is Miss Hackett."

The woman nodded timidly. She wore no makeup and a shapeless matronlike dress. From her unlined face I guessed her age to be close to mine—late thirties—but her gestures and movements were those of an older woman. Hattie Beaumont had called her "Miss" Hackett. She wore no jewelry or rings of any kind. A pair of thick spectacles hung from a chain around her neck. "How do you do?" she said. Her voice was flat, uninflected.

"Hello."

"Miss Hackett manages the household staff. She is also my companion in the true sense of the word, Mr. Rhineheart. In many ways she is closer to me than members of my own family. I depend upon her a great deal." Hattie Beaumont waved a hand at the woman. "You go sit down and let Diane pour the tea."

Miss Hackett nodded and took a seat on a nearby couch. The blond-haired woman came up, leaned down and kissed Hattie Beaumont on the cheek, then turned to me. I stood up and stuck out my hand. She grasped it with the sure, firm grip of a tennis player.

"I'm Michael Rhineheart."

THE QUEEN'S MARE

"Diane Carter. May I call you 'Michael'?"

"Sure."

"Call me 'Diane.'"

She was a nice-looking woman, a slim, cool blond with a nice tan, gray-green eyes, and a brisk, direct way about her that was attractive. It was the second week of May, which meant the tan had been acquired in Florida or courtesy of a tanning salon. Either way, it looked good.

After I sat down, she picked a teacup off the tray and said, "Do you take sugar, Michael?"

I noticed that when she bent down over the tea things, the dress fitted itself to all the right parts of her body. It was a body that didn't appear to have any wrong parts.

"Michael?"

"Huh?"

"Do you take sugar?"

"Uh . . . yes."

"One spoon or two?"

"One."

"Lemon?"

"No thank you."

"Milk?"

"Please."

She handed me my tea, fixed cups for Mrs. Beaumont, Miss Hackett, and herself, then sat down in a nearby chair.

Hattie Beaumont said, "Diane is my right arm, Mr. Rhineheart. In addition to running the day-to-day operations here on the farm, she is a close friend and trusted adviser. She has enormous organizational ability and is quite intelligent. She has a very independent spirit, as I am sure you will discover. She is very frank and candid and is apt to say exactly how she feels. She resembles you in that respect, Mr. Rhineheart. She knows, of course, about everything that's happened so far. So does Meg, of course."

I glanced over at Miss Hackett, who held a pair of needles in her hands. A sewing basket sat in her lap. She seemed oblivious of the conversation, but something told she was listening to every word we said.

Diane Carter addressed her employer. "Have you given Mr. Rhineheart our list of suspects yet?"

FOUR

A pained look crossed Hattie Beaumont's face. She essayed a brief laugh, but it came across as thin and uncomfortable. "Diane is more or less joking, Mr. Rhineheart. We have no list of suspects. It's true that we have done some speculating, but we have no real evidence and"—she turned to Diane—"my dear, you are not seriously suggesting we tell Mr. Rhineheart about our suspicions, are you?"

"Why not?"

Hattie Beaumont spread out her hands. "Well, it's just... I mean... it would be in the nature of guesswork... we have no valid foundation... these are allegations and they involve—" She broke off.

"I'm not sure I agree," Diane Carter said. "I think there's plenty of foundation and that Mr. Rhineheart ought to be informed about everything, including our suspicions." She turned to me. "What do *you* think, Michael?"

I said, "I need all the help I can get." In my head I was trying out various combinations to complete Hattie Beaumont's sentence: These allegations involve... important people?... trusted employees?... members of the... family?

Hattie Beaumont sat silently. After a moment, she shook her head firmly and said, "No, I'm afraid not. I can't allow a matter of such gravity to be reduced to the level of idle conjecture. Perhaps, later, if and when some real evidence turns up... Until then, Mr. Rhineheart, you are going to have to operate without our speculations in this matter."

She turned to her operations director. "Diane, one of your most valuable traits as a friend *and* as an employee is your honesty and independence, and I never want you to hesitate in saying what you feel about any issue, but on this matter, my decision is firm. Are we understood on that?" Hattie Beaumont's gaze was steady and some of the flint crept into her voice.

Diane Carter did not answer immediately. She stared at Hattie, then averted her eyes, and said, "Yes, of course." If what I had been witnessing was a small power struggle, then Diane Carter had come out on the losing end.

Hattie Beaumont returned her attention to me. "In truth, Mr. Rhineheart, whoever was behind the theft is in some ways beside the point. My most pressing and immediate concern is the safe return of the mare and the foal. Let's all of us remember that that is what is paramount here. And also the reason I have need of your services, Mr. Rhineheart. I suggest that we concentrate all our efforts on the ransom exchange. Is that agreeable to you?"

"Sure," I said. I had the feeling that I would find out about their suspicions soon enough.

"Shall I tell you about the theft then?" she said. "The actual details."

How did you answer a question worded like that? "You shall"? "That'd be fine," I said.

"Is that important?" Diane Carter asked. "I mean, if we're going to focus on the ransom, does it really make any difference about the details of the theft?"

"Good point," Hattie Beaumont said.

"The details may or may not turn out to be important," I said, "but I'd still like to hear how it took place."

"Very well," Hattie Beaumont said. She took a small

THE QUEEN'S MARE

sip of tea, set down her cup, then rocked back in her chair. After a moment she launched into an account of the theft.

The thieves, it seems, had driven onto the farm in a pickup truck to which a two-stall horse van was hitched. They were stopped at the main entrance by Eddie Walker, an assistant groom, who was doubling as the main entrance gate guard that evening. He did not recognize the truck or its occupants. According to Walker there were three people in the truck. An older man and two younger men. When he asked them what they wanted, the older man pulled a gun on Walker and together with one of the younger men forced him into the guard cubicle. Walker had tried to resist and was knocked down and kicked in the side. The thieves tied his hands and feet with strong ropes and left him in the cubicle, bound and gagged. They then, apparently, made their way to the foaling barn, where from the evidence of the tire tracks, they backed the van up to Winterset's stall, took the mare and the foal, and made their escape—probably, Hattie said, the same way they had entered—through the main gate.

I took a sip of tea. It was pretty good. Definitely not tea-bag stuff. The cup, I noticed, had a flower pattern on it. I couldn't recognize what species. It might have been a rose. On the other hand, it could have been a violet. I'm not good on flowers.

I tried to remember the last time I had been to a tea party. The fifth grade, probably, at Saint Joseph's, in the West End of Louisville. Sister Mary Hope called them "tea socials" and said you never knew when learning how to behave at an afternoon tea social was going to come in handy. The funny thing is she might have been right. I wondered what the good sister would have made of this odd group of tea sippers. The Mistress of Ashtree Farms, her beautiful young operations person, the servant-companion on the couch, and the sleazy private eye in the wrinkled sport coat.

The rocking chair creaked slightly as Hattie Beaumont resumed her story. While the theft was taking place, the barn watchman had been distracted by a small brushfire that had flared up in the north pasture. The north pasture was, Hattie Beaumont pointed out, some distance from the foaling barn and the other barns and farm buildings.

The brushfire was quickly extinguished. When the barn watchman returned to the foaling barn and discovered that Winterset and the foal were gone, he telephoned Hattie Beaumont immediately. Hattie woke Diane, who was spending the night on the farm—in an apartment above the carriage house, and together, they drove down from the house. In searching the area, one of the first things they did, of course, was to check on the guard station at the main entrance, where they found Walker bound and gagged. Walker told them what had happened.

"It was at that point," Hattie Beaumont said, "that Diane and I realized that the mare and the foal had been stolen. I am not an overly emotional woman, Mr. Rhineheart. Nor am I what you would call a weak sister. Neither is Diane. But at that exact moment both of us burst into tears."

Hattie Beaumont and Diane Carter exchanged commiserating looks, and for a moment I was afraid that they were going to repeat the tearful scene in front of me. There are a couple of scenes that give me real trouble. One of them is a woman in tears. The possibility of two women weeping at the same time was what made me jump in and say, "Did either of you happen to notice what time it was?"

Diane Carter looked puzzled by the question, but Hattie Beaumont nodded and said, "Yes, as a matter of fact. I peeked at my watch. It was 3:35 A.M. on Sunday morning."

FIVE

I nodded and took another swallow of tea. One gate guard and one night watchman didn't seem like enough protection for a 6,000-acre horse farm, but I held back from asking Hattie Beaumont who had drawn up Ashtree's security plan. It was a question I decided to save for another time. Instead, I said, "Tell me about the gate guard. Eddie . . . ?"

"Walker," Diane said. "What about him?"

"How long has he worked here?"

"A little over a year, I believe. I'd have to check his personnel records to be sure."

"Is he a good employee . . . dependable?"

"He seems to be, yes."

"Any chance he's lying? Is it possible he was involved in the theft?"

Diane Carter and Hattie Beaumont looked at each other. Diane shook her head. "I don't think so, no."

"When you found him in the guard station, was there anything suspicious?"

"No. Quite the contrary," Diane said. "His forehead was bleeding and he appeared to be tightly bound."

She looked to Hattie, who nodded confirmingly and said, "Yes, that's correct."

Diane Carter said, "There doesn't seem to be any reason to suspect Eddie Walker."

I didn't tell her that was the wrong way to operate.

I didn't say that in the detective trade you needed reasons *not* to suspect people.

"We get all our farm help through the services of the Thoroughbred Employment Agency," Hattie Beaumont said. "I understand that they screen all their applicants quite thoroughly." She turned to her operations director. "Isn't that so, Diane?"

Diane Carter said, "They have an excellent reputation."

"I'm sure they do," I said, "but I'm going to want to talk to Walker. Is he around?"

"Eddie's off today," Diane Carter said. "I believe he has an apartment in the Saint Matthews area. I have his phone number, and if you like, I'll give him a call when we're finished and tell him you want to speak to him."

"I'd appreciate that," I said. I turned to Hattie Beaumont. "Tell me about the ransom call."

"I answered the phone," Hattie Beaumont said. "Diane was not here. Neither was Meg. It was a man. He spoke in a muffled way. I'm not sure how to describe his voice. It was as if he were speaking through some device or as if he had something in his mouth. He was strange-sounding and hard to understand, and yet I have this feeling that I have heard the voice somewhere before."

"What do you mean by that?" I asked.

"I'm not sure, Mr. Rhineheart. There was something ... I don't know ... familiar about the voice."

"Was it the voice of someone you've spoken to— either on the phone, or in person?"

"I don't know." She shook her head in confusion. "I'm not sure."

"What did he say?" I asked.

"He said he had the mare and the foal and that both were in good shape and not being harmed. He said they were in the hands of people who knew horses and would be taken care of and not hurt unless I failed to comply with their demands."

"Did he use the word *comply*?"

Hattie Beaumont frowned, as if the question had confused her. "I'm not sure. I don't think so."

"Go on," I said.

"He told me to get the million dollars together in used one-hundred-dollar bills and to wait until he called, at which time, there would be, he said, further instructions."

"Did he say when he would call?"

"I got the impression that it would be soon, within the next few days."

"Did he say anything else?"

"He advised me not to tell the police about the ransom, and he warned me not to mark the bills in any way. Then he suggested that I employ someone to handle the exchange arrangements. He said that things would proceed more smoothly if I used someone who had some experience in these matters and who knew what he was doing. That was when *your* name came up, Mr. Rhineheart."

I had the cup raised to my lips and was getting ready to take another swallow of tea when she said that. I set the cup down on the serving cart and sat up straight. "The *thief* mentioned my name?"

"I don't recall exactly," Hattie Beaumont said. "I'm not sure of the exact context in which your name came up. I may have asked him if he had any suggestions about whom to employ. In any case, he seemed quite familiar with your, uh, exploits, Mr. Rhineheart. Apparently, he'd read about you in the newspapers. He said he'd heard that you were experienced in ransom exchanges, and that you could be trusted to follow orders and keep your mouth shut."

I looked over at Diane Carter, who was covering her mouth with her hand, trying to hide a smile, and not doing a very good job of it.

"Mrs. Beaumont," I said slowly, "the message I'm getting is that I've been hired on the recommendation of the people who stole your mare and the foal. Is that right?"

"No, of course not," she said. "Your name might have been mentioned by the thief, but it was also known to me, to us. You are rather well known among horse people, sir. Isn't that right, Diane?"

"Oh, absolutely," Diane Wakefield said. *Droll* was the only word for her tone.

"And whether you know it or not, Mr. Rhineheart, your reputation is quite outstanding in the Thoroughbred breeding industry."

"Yes indeed," Diane Carter said with a twinkle in her eye. "We had you checked out, Michael. Surreptitiously, but thoroughly. The general consensus is that you are quite honest and as good as they come at what you do."

I nodded glumly. Unsolicited praise tends to depress me. I was beginning to wonder why I had agreed so readily to take the case. It did not appear to be any kind of reasonable operation. The thieves held all the cards. There looked to be at least several different ways I could lose on this one.

An overwhelming urge to have a cigarette rose up in me. Automatically, I began searching through my pockets for one, then realized in the midst of the search that I had quit smoking a month ago. I took my hands out of my pockets, balled them up into fists, and propped them on my knees.

"Let's talk about the money," I said.

Hattie Beaumont nodded. "The one million dollars is being put together the way the thief requested. Ashtree's attorney, Wallace Thornton, is seeing to that. I will call Wallace and arrange for you to meet with him this afternoon. His office is in downtown Louisville."

I tried to picture the million being put together. How many hundred-dollar bills in a million? How much space did it take up? Would it fit into a large suitcase? A medium-sized one?

"Wallace will be under instructions to cooperate with you fully, Mr. Rhineheart. He will handle all the details of securing the money, and will be ready to transfer it to you at the proper time." Hattie Beaumont cleared her throat. "There are several other things we need to talk about," she said. "The matter, for one, of Winterset's ownership."

I remembered Paige's earlier remark. "The mare doesn't belong to you then?"

"That's correct," Hattie Beaumont said. "She boards here."

"Does it make any difference who owns her?" I asked.

Hattie Beaumont and Diane Carter exchanged looks.

"Ordinarily," Hattie Beaumont said, "I would say it wouldn't. But this is a slightly different situation. This is no ordinary owner. You see, Winterset belongs to the Queen."

The Queen? What was she talking about? I looked over at Diane Carter, who was smiling brightly at me. I turned back to Hattie Beaumont. "What queen are you talking about?"

"The Queen of England," Hattie Beaumont said.

I looked at her face. She didn't seem to be joking. *The Queen of England?*

"And there is something else," Hattie Beaumont said.

Something else? What else could there possibly be? I was already on the edge of my chair, but I managed to lean forward.

"She will be here on Sunday," Hattie Beaumont said.

"She?"

"The Queen, of course."

"The Queen will be *here*? On *Sunday*? You mean *this* Sunday? Six days from now?"

Hattie Beaumont nodded. "The visit has been

planned for months. She is coming to see her favorite mare and her new foal, of course."

I picked up my teacup, then set it back down on the tray. There was a plate of cookies on the tray. The cookies were small, round and tan colored. It was the first time I had noticed them.

Hattie Beaumont must have seen me eyeing the cookies. She gestured at them. "Would you like a ginger snap, Mr. Rhineheart?"

I said the first thing that came into my mind: "Of course."

SIX

EDDIE Walker was tall and thin with thick curly black hair, chiseled features, and cold gray eyes that didn't reveal much. He looked to be in his mid-thirties, or better, and the lines around his eyes and in his face suggested that he had been a few places and done a few things. He was dressed in faded jeans and cowboy boots and a powder blue chambray shirt. His knuckles were bandaged and there was a small cut above his right eyebrow. He was seated on a couch in the front room of his apartment, drinking beer out of a can.

The couch was flanked by two end tables containing imitation brass lamps. On the farthest end table was a framed photograph of a pretty sandy-haired woman. The photograph was inscribed in large letters: *To Eddie, from your loving wife, Betty*.

I perched in an armchair across from Walker. To my right the door to the bedroom stood open and I could see the corner of an unmade bed and the edge of a dresser. The private-eye manual says come on strong when it's called for.

"You got no manners, Eddie?"

Eddie looked surprised.

"Somebody comes by you don't offer them a drink, or a cup of tea, or something?"

"A cup of *tea*?"

"Out of courtesy."

Eddie laughed. "For a minute I thought you was serious." He took a pull at his beer.

I scanned his face. The man didn't know any better. "Eddie, you're dumber than you look, aren't you?"

Eddie slapped his knee and guffawed. "Hoo, boy, you a funny man. I thought Miz Wakefield said you was gonna ask me some questions. She said to cooperate with you."

"It's good advice, Eddie."

"You ain't no policeman, though."

"I'm private."

"I could tell you was no real policeman," Eddie said proudly. "I can usually tell a real cop."

"How come?"

"Huh?"

"How can you tell a real cop from a private one."

He smiled slyly. "There's ways."

"You had a lot of experience with real cops, Eddie? Is that why you can tell the difference?"

Eddie took a long swig of beer. He looked at me coldly, then he laughed and shook his head. "Naw, hell, I ain't got no experience with cops. Truth is I don't know nothing about them. I just pop off a lot, that's all." He took another drink and set the beer can down on the coffee table. "What was it you wanted to ask me about?"

I told Eddie that I wanted him to tell me about the events of Saturday night and Sunday morning. How it took place. From beginning to end. Everything he could remember.

Eddie said, yeah, sure, he would try his best to remember exactly how it all had happened. He pulled a pack of Camel filters out of his shirt pocket and offered me one. I shook my head and he whipped out a Zippo, lit up, and blew out a cloud of smoke. Then he sat back on the couch and began to talk. His account of what had happened was the same as Hattie Beaumont's, only more elaborate. The pickup truck was a blue Chevy four-wheel drive, '85 or '86 model, with the large cab. The horse van was a twenty-foot Mack trailer, yellow. The gun that had been pointed at him was a .38 Smith & Wesson with a long barrel.

He described the thieves in some detail. The two young ones looked to be in their twenties. They wore caps. One had a beard. The other was fat, round faced. The older man had gray hair, bad teeth, a raspy voice. The young ones had not talked at all. The older man had given directions. Do this. Go here. Hold him still. Yes, he would probably recognize the older one's voice if he heard it again. He had struggled when they began to tie him up and the older one had knocked him down and kicked him in the side.

Walker rubbed his side. His ribs were *still* sore. The thieves had left him tied up like a fucking hog or something in the guard station. They had stuffed a gag in his mouth and he had spent the next two or three hours trying to untie himself. Bound up like that and on the floor of the guard station, he hadn't seen or heard anything. The next thing that happened was when Mrs. Beaumont and Miss Carter came into the station and found him. He told them what had happened and they told him about the missing mare and foal. They'd asked him not to tell the police or anyone else about the theft and that was fine with him. A little while ago, Miss Carter had called him and asked him to answer all my questions regarding the theft. Which was no problem. He just hoped he'd been helpful, he said.

He jabbed his cigarette out in a butt-filled ashtray, picked up his beer, sipped it, and eyed me with a look I'd seen professional card dealers bestow on blackjack players.

My opinion of Eddie's intelligence had risen a notch. The story he'd just related was a real prize. It was conceivable, logical, entirely possible, but there was also something a little too pat and ready-made about it, as if it had been rehearsed.

One of the problems of living in this world is that there are times when you want to call someone a motherfucking liar and sucker-punch them but you have to do the opposite and be nice.

"You *have* been helpful, Eddie," I said in the voice of a car salesman, "and I appreciate it. I really do."

"I'm just glad I could help some," Eddie said in the same tone.

"I want to ask you a few more questions."

"Sure. Go 'head."

"How long you been with Ashtree?"

"Little over a year."

"What's your job title?"

"Assistant head groom, but I do exactly the same things the head groom does. Exact same responsibilities."

"How'd you get your job?"

"Through Thoroughbred Employment."

"Where'd you work before?"

"At Brookview Farms. Over in Lexington."

"Before that?"

"Before that I walked hots for Jack Kruger."

"You been in the horse business long, Eddie?"

"Ten years. I done other things, too, but I really like working with Thoroughbreds."

"You ever been in trouble with the law?"

There was a momentary hesitation. "Drinkin' and fightin' is all."

"You been in the military, Eddie?"

"Three years in the navy."

I nodded at the photograph on the end table. "Your wife?"

"Ex."

I leaned forward and put an earnest look on my face. I didn't want to lay it on too thick, but I wanted Eddie to get the impression that I was truly interested in his opinion. Playing dumb came fairly naturally to me.

"Eddie, you got any idea who might be behind the kidnapping?"

He shook his head. "I sure don't."

I took a business card out of my pocket and handed it to him. "If you think of something, or get an idea about the case, or hear anything, I want you to call me. All right?"

"I sure will." He tucked the card into his shirt pocket.

I rose to my feet. "Eddie, I want to thank you for everything."

Walker jumped up and thrust out his hand. "Like I said," he said, "I'm just glad to help."

I grabbed his hand and pumped it up and down like I was drawing water from a well. We stood there with fake smiles on our faces eyeing each other like two counterpunchers looking for an opening.

SEVEN

WALLACE Thornton was a pale, grim man in a pinstriped Brooks Brothers suit and a silk tie. His office was elegant: mahogany desk, thick carpeting, wood paneling, leather chairs. Outside the window, the muffled sound of downtown Louisville traffic could be heard. Stiff and still, Thornton sat behind his desk. I sprawled in an armchair across from him.

Thornton held out his hand, palm up. "May I see your license, please?"

I dug my wallet out of my pocket and passed it across the desk. Thornton squinted at the license for several moments before he handed it back. "Everything seems in order," he said. "I suppose I ought to tell you at the outset, Mr. Rhineheart, that I advised against using your services in this matter. My initial recommendation to Mrs. Beaumont was that she call the proper authorities. When that was rejected I suggested she use the services of a large security firm with ample resources. That was also rejected, I'm afraid."

He laced his fingers together, set them down on the desk. His gestures were all brief and economical, as if anything more elaborate might cost him some money. "I'm aware of your reputation in certain circles, but frankly, I am not impressed. I have my doubts as to your ability to handle a matter of this gravity and importance on your own. You are, I understand, something of a one-man gang. By that I mean that you usually operate entirely on your own. Is that correct?"

I nodded. "More or less."

"I mentioned your name to someone in a command position with the local police. The phrase 'a loose gun' was used to describe you."

"Isn't that catchy?" I said in my most polite and civil tone. I didn't like Thornton's manner or attitude, but I was determined to be cool and not lose my temper.

"One million dollars is a very large sum of money, Mr. Rhineheart. Does it occur to you that you may be out of your depth?"

I smiled politely. "Yes."

"What would you say to some assistance?"

"What do you mean? What kind of assistance?"

"George Greathouse, a good friend of mine, is the area director of..." Thornton uttered the name of the firm whose guards were now providing Ashtree's security. "The day after the theft I called George's firm in. They've sealed the place up tight. It's quite an organization, Mr. Rhineheart, and George can supply us with five well-trained operatives on very short notice."

I thought about it for two seconds, then shook my head. "I don't work well with groups, or with people I don't know. Aside from that, the thieves won't go for dealing with a *team*. When the thing comes down, they'll want me to come by myself. And if the thieves are any good, they'll be watching to make sure no one is following me at a discreet distance."

"But surely you need some sort of backup or support?"

"Maybe," I said. Thornton had a point. It was possible that in the course of things I would need a good backup man. If so, I knew just who I wanted in that position. A Louisville private eye named Richard Farnsworth, who had forgotten more about the investigator's trade than I would ever learn. Old enough to be somebody's great-grandfather, Farnsworth collected social security and called himself semiretired, but maintained a sleazy little office on Jefferson Street in downtown Louisville. The last time we had worked together was on a case that involved an attempt to fix the Kentucky Derby. In a backup role, Farnsworth had come through like the old pro he was and had saved my ass. "If it turns out I need any help, Counselor," I said to Thornton, "I've got my own people."

"Very well," Thornton said. "Mrs. Beaumont instructed me to cooperate with you, and I intend to do that. I am prepared to answer any questions you might have, offer you whatever assistance you might need."

"I guess my first question," I said, "is whether you have any idea who might be behind the theft of the horses and the ransom demand?"

Thornton gazed past my shoulder at nothing in particular. "No," he said, "of course not. Not the slightest idea."

He's lying, I thought. I wondered why, but I wasn't surprised. Once a case began, everyone began to lie. Sometimes they lied when they could just as easily have told the truth. There was something about being a private eye that brought out the lies and the liars in people.

"In any case," Thornton said, "isn't that line of inquiry really outside the scope of your assignment, Mr. Rhineheart?"

"What scope are you talking about, Counselor?"

"It's my understanding that your role in this is more or less limited to acting as a kind of go-between during the ransom exchange. Correct me," he said, "if I'm wrong about that."

"You're not wrong," I said. "My main job is to see to the safe return of the mare and the foal. On the other hand, the more I know about things, the better I'm able to operate. I thought that maybe you might be able to help me out in that respect, Counselor."

"I'm afraid I don't quite follow. In what way might I be able to help?"

I shrugged. I was feeling around in the dark. "You

might know something I don't know. In view of your long association with Ashtree Farms and Mrs. Beaumont, you might be in possession of some information that might be helpful."

"What kind of information?" Thornton was playing it a little too dumb.

I shrugged. "I don't know. For example," I said, "it might help me to know who Mrs. Beaumont's enemies are."

Thornton raised an eyebrow. "Enemies?"

"Yeah," I said. "Business enemies, personal enemies. You don't build an organization as big and as important as Ashtree without making some enemies."

"Isn't that a bit melodramatic?"

I shrugged. "No more melodramatic than paying a million dollars to ransom some kidnapped Thoroughbreds is."

Thornton raised his fist to his mouth and coughed quietly into it. "Well, I wish I could help you, Mr. Rhineheart, but I know of nothing that I think would help you carry out your assignment. And I'm afraid I don't see what all this has to do with how you're going to negotiate the details of the ransom exchange. It seems to me your instructions are quite clear on the extent of your responsibilities."

Thornton was right. The only problem was that I wasn't very good at following instructions. "I understand there's a power struggle going on at Ashtree, a plot to unseat Mrs. Beaumont as the chief executive officer. What about that?"

Thornton waved a hand. The gesture was dismissive. "I don't know where you're getting your information, but it's erroneous."

"My source was Mrs. Beaumont herself."

Thornton grunted. "As you might have discovered for yourself, Mrs. Beaumont is getting on in years. She's made some management decisions in recent years that have not sat well with all the shareholders. As a result the board has divided into several factions. A number of significant people oppose Hattie's policies. They are shareholders and have a right to their own views. It's strictly a matter of business. There's hardly a plot, sir."

"Which faction do you belong to?"

Thornton smiled coldly. "None of your business."

"Fair enough," I said. "My only other question has to do with the money," I said. "Is it ready?"

Thornton nodded. "It is at this moment on the premises of the First Central Bank of Kentucky. I can take possession of it on thirty minutes notice any time of the day or night. I would then be prepared to turn it over to you at your request."

"Any chance of a leak to the newspeople or to the cops from the bank personnel?"

Thornton shook his head. "This is all being handled at the highest levels."

Yeah. And when the money was transferred to me it would begin its descent down to one of the lower levels. The level where the ransom exchange would take place. The level of the thieves and whoever had to deal with them. The level where you had to get your hands in it. I thought about saying all this to Thornton, but decided there was no real reason to. I stood up. It was time to head back to the office and go to work.

"Before you leave, Mr. Rhineheart, let me ask you something."

"Sure."

"In regard to the ransom exchange, what is your basic game plan?"

"Game plan?"

"Yes. Surely you have a plan of some sort. Some overall concept of how the exchange is going to develop, the possible courses of action that are available, depending, of course, on the behavior of the thieves."

I shrugged. "I don't have any plan. This is not an N.F.L game, Counselor. When the thieves call, I'll see what they want to do, then play it by ear."

THE QUEEN'S MARE

Thornton frowned, displaying his displeasure with my answer.

"What about the money, Mr. Rhineheart? I know what the thieves' instructions were, but shouldn't we make some attempt to mark it?"

I shrugged. "I don't know. Who would we get to mark it? Without bringing in the cops, that is? Your high-level people know how to mark money so it can be traced?"

Thornton shook his head. "I have no idea. I suppose I can find out."

"Check it out," I said. "I've got no objection to marking the money, if it doesn't mess up the exchange. See what your boss has to say."

Another frown creased Thornton's forehead. "When you say 'boss,' Mr. Rhineheart, are you referring to Mrs. Beaumont?"

"You got other bosses?"

"Sir, I am afraid you don't understand exactly what's involved in a legal relationship. Mrs. Beaumont is not my 'boss' in any sense of the word." A plastic box on Thornton's desk began to buzz. He looked annoyed at this interruption, as if this meant he wouldn't get a chance to explain the difference between *boss* and *client*.

He punched a button on the box and in a curt voice said, "What is it, Jenny?"

"Ms. Charlotte Beaumont is here, sir. She says she has to see you this minute. She won't wait. She—"

The office door flew open with a theatrically loud thud. A tall beautiful woman wearing an off-the-shoulder expensive-looking dress came striding into the room. She was an older, and, if it was possible, a more attractive version of her daughter, Paige. They looked a good deal alike. Charlotte was an inch taller, five pounds heavier, her eyes deep and dark, her mouth a wide sexy slit in a classically featured face. The difference might have been in the sexual glow she gave off, a heat that I could feel all the way on the other side of the room. Her hair was a lighter color than Paige's but an equally snarled and luxurious mass of curls and ringlets. Her eyes, which were almond shaped, burned with intensity.

"Wallace," she declaimed loudly, "Wallace, I want you to inform me just what in the gawdamn hell is going on. I have been given to understand that Mama has hired herself a private detective, of all things. Is that correct?"

Her voice was like an instrument, full of shadings and tones that carried to all the corners of the room. She had the barest trace of a Southern accent.

She had reached the general area of the desk and came to a halt when she spotted me. She cocked her head to one side and gave me a cool and thorough assessment, as if she was checking out something she was about to buy.

Her lips formed a circle. "Who," she asked, "are you?"

I made no reply. I didn't smile. I just stared at her. The truth is I couldn't take my eyes off her.

Charlotte Beaumont frowned. It was clear that she was not used to anyone not responding to her promptly and immediately.

Wallace Thornton looked uncomfortable. "Charlotte," he said, "this is Mr. Rhineheart. He was just preparing to leave."

"You're the private detective," she said, fixing her eyes on me.

I nodded.

"I don't believe I've ever met a private eye before," Charlotte said. "Socially, that is."

"You haven't missed much," I said.

"Of course," she continued, "my ex-husband used to employ them by the dozen to spy on me. So that's not to say I haven't encountered one or two. On the business level." She flashed a dazzling smile my way.

"But that's not the same thing, is it, Mr. Rhineheart?"

"Not exactly."

"I like your name. Rhineheart. It's German, isn't it? What's it mean?"

"I have no idea."

"Split spirit, divided soul, something like that. What's your first name?"

"Michael."

"One of the great loves of my life was named Michael," she said, then suddenly asked, "What do you think of Mama?" Her abrupt conversational changes reminded me of Paige.

"She's quite a woman," I said.

"I call her 'Mama,' but she's not really my mama. She's *far* too old to be my real mother. My real mother is dead. Hattie is my grandmother."

"You look far too young to be her granddaughter," I said.

Charlotte rewarded this remark with another brilliant smile. "You're quite clever, Michael. And you're right. I *am* too young to be her granddaughter. Nevertheless, it's true. My mother and father were killed in a tragic automobile accident twenty-five years ago. I was a mere child then." She turned to see Thornton holding a chair for her. "Oh, do sit down, Wallace," she said impatiently. "Can't you see that Mr. Rhineheart and I are having a discussion?"

Thornton flushed, but otherwise managed to look as grim as ever.

"Where were we?" Charlotte said to me.

"We were talking about your grandmother."

"Oh yes, and you're absolutely right. She is quite a woman. Twenty-five years ago she *rode to hounds*. Can you imagine that? When she was younger and Granddaddy was still alive, she went on a big-game safari to Africa. Bagged a rhino, the story goes. Of course, she's getting rather old now. There was a time when she ran Ashtree Farms with an iron hand, but those days are long gone." She turned to Thornton again. "Aren't they, Wallace?"

"Whatever you say, Charlotte."

Charlotte reached out and touched my arm. "Wallace patronizes me. He thinks I'm dumb and that I talk too much."

Thornton's voice was impatient. "Charlotte, please."

Charlotte Beaumont ignored him. "What do you think of Wallace?" she asked me. "He's a stick, isn't he?"

I let that pass.

"I attribute Mama's current decline to the accident," Charlotte said. "I believe the trauma of it all just buried itself in her subconscious for twenty-five years and is just emerging. Which is the main reason she has been behaving so irrationally of late. Seeing plots where none exist. Letting Ashtree go into decline."

"Charlotte!"

Charlotte turned and gave Thornton a withering look, then turned back to me. "Have you been out to the farm and met Diane Carter and Miss Hackett and all the household staff yet?"

"More or less," I said. "I met your daughter, too," I added.

"Paige? What did you think of her, Mr. Rhineheart? As a future adult, I mean, does she have any potential?" She waved a hand quickly. "Never mind. Don't answer that. Have you met my sister Shirley yet?"

"I haven't had the pleasure," I said.

"It's no pleasure," Charlotte said, "believe me. She is more than several years older than me, a sexual deviate, and a nastier, meaner, back-stabbing bitch of a person than I wouldn't wish as a sister on a full-fledged enemy of mine." Her voice shifted abruptly again. Confidentiality was the newest tone. "I understand," she whispered, "that an Ashtree mare and its foal have been kidnapped."

I put a blank look on my face.

THE QUEEN'S MARE

Charlotte favored me with another smile. "You don't talk a whole lot. I like that in a man. You and I need to get together privately, Mr. Rhineheart. Do you have a card, or something?"

I took a card out of my wallet and handed it to her. It was the plain card without the trench coat and the Python.

"I see your office is on Main Street," she said. "Isn't that a fortunate coincidence. I'm right down the block at the Center for the Arts. I'm currently starring in a production of *The Sea Gull* by Chekov. We open this coming Saturday. Are you familiar with Chekov, Mr. Rhineheart?"

"Not very," Rhineheart said.

"I bet you've never seen me act, either," she said, as if that was even worse than not knowing Chekov.

"I'm afraid I haven't."

"You ought to be 'shamed of yourself," Charlotte said. She shook a reproving finger. "You going to have to make up for that. Take me to dinner, or something. I'm staying at the Seelbach, Mr. Rhineheart. The Presidential Suite. Call me."

She held out her hand. I was being dismissed.

I took her hand and gave it a brief squeeze. On my way out of the room, I passed Thornton, who was glowering at me.

"Don't look so upset, Counselor," I said. "I'll be back in touch and you can tell me the difference between *clients* and *bosses*."

EIGHT

I drove from Thornton's office directly over to Farnsworth's place. Main to Third. Third to Jefferson, where I grabbed a right and parked in front of the Peeping Eye Movie Theater. Farnsworth's rat hole of an office was on the second floor, above the Jefferson Street Cafe & Lounge, a topless bar.

Farnsworth was seated behind his desk. I hadn't seen him for a while, but he hadn't changed. The same narrow face and sharp features, the same beady little eyes that reminded me of an alert rat. His hair was the same color—tobacco brown peppered with gray—and texture—thin, lank—and he combed it the same way—straight back from his forehead. He even looked to be wearing the same shiny brown suit that he had on the last time I'd seen him.

"Pull up a chair, kid." Farnsworth indicated a black wooden chair that looked like it belonged in a kitchen. It and the desk and Farnsworth's chair and a mustard-colored couch were the only furniture. All of it looked like it came from the Goodwill used-furniture sale. "What's up?"

I told Farnsworth I'd just finished talking to someone who'd called me a one-man gang.

"Sounds like he knows you well," Farnsworth said. "What else is new?"

"Some serious shit," I said.

"How serious?"

THE QUEEN'S MARE

"Blooded horses," I said. "Ransoms fit for a king. Stuff like that."

"Sounds inneresting," Farnsworth said. "Fill me in."

"You know Ashtree Farms?"

Farnsworth smiled, displaying a badly fitted set of dentures. "An old handicapper like me? That's like asking a wino if he's ever heard of Ernest and Julio Gallo. Ashtree's Hattie Beaumont's place."

I nodded. "The other night a broodmare named Winterset was kidnapped off the farm. The thieves got a foal just dropped by the mare, and both of them belong to the Queen of England."

Farnsworth, normally a dead pan, lifted his eyebrows in surprise. "*Who?*"

"The Queen of England."

"You serious?"

"Dead serious."

"You talking about Elizabeth the Ninth, or whoever?"

"That's right. Except I think she's the Second."

"You're kidding me, aren't you?"

"I wish I was, old man. This is the straight stuff. The foal was sired by BuckMaster."

"BuckMaster? You're talking big-time breeding fees. Valuable horseflesh."

"The thieves want a cool million in ransom."

"Sweet Jesus," Farnsworth said with feeling. He got up out of his chair, came around the desk, walked over to the door, opened it, looked out in the hallway, shut the door, then walked back behind the desk. He remained standing. "A million dollars?" he said.

I nodded. "And I'm the delivery boy."

"What's my job?" Farnsworth asked.

"Sit down, old man," I said, "that's what I'm here to tell you about."

"Bullshit."

"I swear to God, McGraw."

"The Queen of England, huh?"

"Cross my heart and hope to die."

McGraw shook her head. "I don't believe it," she said. "I don't believe the stuff about the tea and cookies, either. I think you made this all up."

"Have it your own way." I laid the four-figure retainer Hattie Beaumont had given me down on McGraw's desk, walked over to mine, sat down, and propped up my feet.

McGraw picked up the check and studied it carefully. "This appears to be real. Does it mean I'll be able to enroll in school next month?"

The school McGraw was referring to was the Southern Police Institute, which was located on the University of Louisville campus. The Institute was offering a course in Investigative Techniques on their summer schedule.

"Deposit it," I said. "Write yourself a check for two weeks back salary and give me the rest."

"Tell me the whole thing again," McGraw said. "From the tea and cookies to the Queen. And don't leave anything out."

"We don't have the time, babe. I need you to do some research for me this afternoon."

"What kind of research?"

"I want everything you can find on Hattie Beaumont, the Beaumont family, and Ashtree Farms. Old newspaper clippings, magazine articles, the works. Look especially for articles that deal with the farm's finances."

"Why are we doing this? I thought the job was just a simple ransom exchange thing."

"It probably is," I said, "but then on the other hand it may turn into something else. You never know."

McGraw made a face. "God, I hate library work."

I shrugged. "It's part of the trade, babe. P.I.s spend a hell of lot more time digging through old records and files than they do going on ransom exchanges."

"Yeah? Then how come I never see *you* in the library?"

"Because," I said, "I got an ace researcher like you doing it for me."

McGraw nodded skeptically. "Uh-huh." She glanced at her watch. "Library closes at six on Tuesdays," she said, and began to rummage through her purse, an oversized oblong lump of gray leather. She withdrew a change purse, a wad of Kleenex, a set of keys, a worn paperback copy of *The Long Goodbye*, a compact case, and finally, a tube of lipstick. She held a mirror up and began to apply the lipstick to her mouth. "By the way," she added, "I've got a date later tonight."

"Good luck to both of you."

"He's taking me to the Vogue," McGraw said, putting the stuff back in her purse. The Vogue was a movie theater on Lexington Road that featured revivals of old movies.

"Don't tell me what's playing," I said. "I'm not interested. I'm probably not going to be able to go to any movies until this thing is over, so don't tell me what's on."

McGraw grabbed up her purse and walked over to the door. She opened it, turned back to me, said, *"On the Waterfront,"* and left.

On the Waterfront. Jesus Christ. Brando. Lee J. Cobb. Rod Steiger. Eva Marie Saint. Shot in black and white. Directed by Elia Kazan. Screenplay by Budd Schulberg. Terry Malloy and Johnny Friendly. The cab scene. "You don't understand... I coulda been a contender..." I'd seen the movie at least twenty times.

I stayed in the office past closing time. I cleaned my weapon, looked through the mail, straightened up my desk, and put in a phone order for a six-pack and a large extra cheese-pepperoni-and-sausage pizza that was delivered by a short fat kid in a checkered uniform. I was on my second beer and halfway through the pizza when I heard footsteps in the hallway outside the office.

There was no reason for anyone to be in the hallway this late. I took my weapon out of its holster, flipped off the safety, and laid it on the desk.

The office door swung open and two men entered. The first one in the door was white, the second black. Both were big and beefy, and both were dressed in sport shirts that hung outside their slacks. The white guy had a mustache. The black guy wore sunglasses.

The black one pointed to the pizza box and said, "Look here, Mac, we got us a pizza lover."

I picked up my weapon and pointed it in their direction. "How can I help you gentlemen?"

"Easy now," the black guy said, holding up a hand. "No need for weapons."

"That's nice to hear," I said, "but what do you call those items that y'all have tucked in your belts?"

The black guy said, "I believe you got the best of us, friend."

"Both of you, put your hands up. Like in the movies."

They looked at each other.

"Don't even think about it," I said, "if you want to remain among the living."

They raised their hands.

"You"—I pointed the Python at the white guy—"keep your hands raised." To the other one I said, "You, you take your piece out slowly by the fingertips and set it on the floor."

"Hey, friend, you talking about my gun now. You don't want to be fuckin' with a man's gun."

I cocked the weapon and sighted. "Do what I tell you, or I'll drop you in your tracks."

"Easy," the black guy said. "Easy." He lifted up his shirt and removed his weapon slowly and carefully and set it on the floor, then put his hands back up in the air.

"You do it the same way," I told the white guy. He

did as he was told. "Now," I said, "how can I help you fellas?"

The black guy seemed to be the spokesman. He said, "Mr. Graves wants to see you."

Mr. Graves? Mr. Graves, whose first name was Curtis, was a successful entrepreneur whose business was crime—drugs and gambling, for the most part. He operated out of the West End of Louisville. Curtis and I were old friends. We were both from the same area of Louisville, had been drafted at the same time, had gone through basic and jump school and infantry training together, and had ended up walking the same patrol in the I Drang Valley.

After the army we had both returned to Louisville. Curtis had gone into crime and had made it big. I had drifted into the private-eye business and was surviving. Although we seldom ran into each other, we had remained friendly. I could think of no reason why Curtis would send his muscle to my office. The next time I saw him I'd have to ask him. "Would that be Mr. Curtis Graves you're talking about?"

"That's him."

"Why's Curtis want to see me?"

"We don't know nothing about that. We just the messengers, man."

I picked up a slab of pizza and took a bite. I chewed it slowly and kept my weapon pointed toward the pair. I washed the food down with a swallow of beer. Then I said, "Tell Curtis that if he wants to see me, he knows where my office is. Tell him I don't appreciate him sending people. Tell him if he wants to see me to come by himself."

The white guy stroked his mustache. The black guy said, "Mr. Graves not going to like that kind of reply."

"That's tough shit," I said. "That's the only kind of reply I got for you." I pointed my weapon at the white guy. "What's your name?"

"Macnamara," he said in a hoarse voice.

I nodded. "I just wanted to see if you could talk." I indicated the door. "It's time to split, fellas."

"What about our weapons?" the black guy said.

I raised my voice. "Move."

They hustled out the door and I could hear their feet tramping down the stairway and the sound of the downstairs door opening and closing.

I took a deep breath and let it out. I thumbed down the hammer, put away my weapon, and thought about my visitors. I told myself it didn't matter, was no big deal. Like low pay and long hours and sleazy clients, threatening visits were part of the game. You couldn't let any of it get to you. On the other hand the pizza didn't look quite as appetizing as it had earlier. I left the rest of it sitting on my desk for the janitor.

It was after seven when I got home. I checked with my answering service—there were no calls on my home number—and fixed myself a pot of Irish tea. I went into the living room and switched on the tube. After a moment, the faces of Humphrey Bogart and Ingrid Bergman formed themselves on the small screen. One of the channels was showing *Casablanca*.

Casablanca had been Catherine's favorite movie. Catherine. In 1976 she was twenty-five years old, a slim beautiful woman with gray eyes and long brown hair that hung down across her shoulders. We had been married for almost a year. She was driving on the expressway, coming downtown to pick me up when a semitrailer-truck jumped the divider and smashed into her car. The driver of the truck had been drinking. Catherine had been three months pregnant.

I got up and snapped off the television and began to wander aimlessly around the apartment. In one of the kitchen cabinets I found a fifth of Old Fitzgerald. Eight years old—86 proof. I threw some ice cubes into a tall glass and poured myself three inches of Kentucky bourbon. Back in the front room I dug out an old Bessie

THE QUEEN'S MARE

Smith album and put it on the box. I sipped bourbon and listened to the music for a while and then around midnight I turned off the stereo and concentrated on the bourbon.

NINE

The next morning I woke up with a headache. My stomach was queasy and I had a bad taste in my mouth. I put on a pair of old gym shorts, a torn sweatshirt, laced up my Adidas, jumped in my car, and drove over to Bellarmine College. A collection of two dozen brick buildings scattered across several acres of grassy hillside, Bellarmine is a small Catholic liberal arts school named after a sixteenth-century priest-scholar. One end of the campus contains tennis courts, a soccer field, a softball diamond, and a quarter-mile running track with a cinder-based surface. It is a pleasant place and draws runners and walkers from all over the city.

On a crowded track I ran for over an hour, and was on my last lap when I looked over at the cars parked along the shoulder of Newburg Road and saw a huge white stretch limo with darkly tinted windows sitting there. Graves's pimpmobile, I thought. Has to be. The car was a kind of trademark. I smiled and walked over. When I was ten feet away the back door swung open automatically with a *swoosh*ing sound like the electric-eye doors in a supermarket. Curtis waved from the corner of the backseat. He was wearing Ray Ban shades and his tightly wired hair was shaped into a rectangle that gave him the look of an Egyptian prince.

He was certainly dressed like a prince. In a cream-colored silk suit cut in the latest fashion, and long pointy green-on-brown suede-on-leather tasseled loafers. The shoes alone looked as if they had cost nine hundred dollars. Graves smiled and held out his cocoa-colored hand when I slid into the backseat. Up front the driver, a black guy with a shaved head, was hunched over the steering wheel, the wire to a Walkman plugged in one ear.

"Curtis, you've turned into a Yuppie since the last time I saw you," I said, taking his hand.

He gripped my fingers in a little sissy shake and said, "This is how they say hello in Beverly Hills, R. How you doing? How come it's such a pleasure to see your big ugly white face, R.?"

I said, "I don't know. Maybe it's for the same reason I'm glad to see that evil grin of yours."

"Man, you don't think we like each other, do you?"

I shrugged. "I don't know. I'd hate to think it was true. But it could be."

Curtis laughed. "Face it, R., we friends. The hustler and the private cop. We don't approve of each other, but for some reason we get along."

"That's going to end though," I said, "you keep sending bad guys to my office."

"I was just going to mention that, R. That visit was what you call premature. I gave out some orders to get in touch with you and they were taken literally. I want to apologize for any inconvenience it might have caused you."

"There's no need to apologize."

Curtis frowned. "I *know* there's no need. I *want* to apologize, R. It's part of my new image, which is modeled after your typical market-oriented entrepreneur." He knotted his paisley tie, smoothed out the lapels of his suit, threw out a cuff-linked arm in a sweeping gesture to include the clothes, his car and driver, the whole routine. "What do you think?"

"I think it's you, Curtis. All the way."

He nodded. "Down to business, R. You been hired to go between a ransom exchange for a mare and the foal 'napped from Ashtree Farms. Don't ask me how I know that. I just do. I'm here to offer you some help."

"Help? What kind of help?"

"Any kind you want. Whatever it takes for you to do your job. You want operational help, some people who know the ins and outs of kidnapping and ransom exchanges, I can put you in touch with them. You need some people to go around and ask questions, you got it. You need some head busters, they're yours. You need some heavy weapons, just gimme a call."

It took me a minute to digest what I'd just heard. An ex-street thief from Thirty-second and Dusmenil was offering to help me stage a ransom for a couple of priceless Thoroughbreds that had been stolen from one of the premier breeding farms in the world. The Thoroughbreds were owned by the Queen of England. I may have had stranger offers in the past, but I couldn't remember them.

"You making this offer because you're good-hearted, or you got some other reason, Curtis?"

Curtis snickered. "Self-interest, R. It's the prime emotion. Let's just say I have an interest in seeing that whatever involves Ashtree Farms goes smoothly."

"You want to be a little more explicit?"

Curtis shook his head. "I done told you too much already. This is a serious offer, R. I want you to take advantage of it. I'm prepared to help in any way you need."

I found myself staring at the driver's earplug, with literally nothing to say in response to Curtis. "I'll tell you what," I managed after a moment, "let me think about your offer, Curtis."

"Don't think too long. Queen gonna be here in a week."

"How do you know all this, Curtis?"

Curtis smirked. "I'm a well-informed businessman." He handed me a card. It was black with red letters below an embossed figure of a fat man in a trench coat.

The letters spelled out GREENSTREETS with a West End address. The initials *CG* were scrawled on the reverse side of the card. "Here, this'll get you three free drinks at my new joint."

I fingered the card. "I didn't know you were in the nightclub business, Curtis."

He shrugged. "It's an investment, R." He held out his hand. "R, it's been nice seeing you again. Keep me posted." We shook hands as my door *swoosh*ed open.

I stepped out of the car and the door closed. The limo engine roared into life, but before the car moved away, the back window came rolling down, and Graves's face appeared. "One more thing, R."

"What's that, Curtis?"

"Tread lightly."

The window shot up and the car surged out into the street like some huge metal monster.

I drove home, showered, shaved, and got dressed. As I was leaving, the phone began to ring. I picked it up and said hello.

"Michael Rhineheart, please," a breezy voice said.

"Speaking."

"Mr. Rhineheart, this is Dan Horner. I'm a staff writer with the *Lexington Herald*, and I'm calling to confirm some information we've received. It has to do with the alleged theft of a broodmare and her foal from Ashtree Farms, which is located just outside of Louisville. Our sources tell us that your detective agency has been hired by Mrs. Hattie Beaumont, the owner of Ashtree, to find the mare and the foal. Can you tell us whether or not this is correct?"

"Is this for a story you're going to print, or . . . ?"

"Well, we're preparing a story for possible publication, but we need to confirm some facts. Are you working for Ashtree Farms?"

"No."

"No?"

"No."

"Are you telling me that your agency is not acting in an investigative capacity for Ashtree Farms?"

"Yes."

"Well, tell me this—"

I interrupted, "What did you say your name was?"

"Horner. I'm with the *Lexington Herald*."

"Mr. Horner, let me have your number. I'm too busy to talk to you now, but I'll get back to you soon."

"If I could just have a few minutes..."

"Your number, Mr. Horner?"

"It's 989-4309, area code 616, but—"

"I'll get back to you, Mr. Horner." I hung up the phone, feeling like a politician. Things were getting bizarre.

I went outside and got in the car and drove down to my office, which is located on Main Street in downtown Louisville. On the second floor of a 19th-century building located around the corner and a couple of blocks up from the court and police headquarters. The whole area is in the process of renovation, and is swarming with upscale types and trend setters and young business people, one of whom has opened a restaurant called The Bistro on the ground floor below my office. The front of the place is all plate glass with tables in the windows and is imposing enough to have driven away all the neighborhood winos and street people.

My office is one large rectangle of a room with elaborate cornicework, a high ceiling, and plenty of windows. You can look out from any angle and see a lot of other old buildings. My notion of a nice view.

My desk is worth seeing, also. It's an old wooden rolltop with plenty of pigeonholes and lots of character. The wall behind it is real brick and cool to the touch. McGraw's desk, a beat-up steel gray job, stands near the door. An old blue-black Royal Standard squats on it. I've come to think of her typewriter as a kind of desk decoration, and was surprised this particular morning to see McGraw pecking away on it.

"What the hell are you doing?"

"What's it look like I'm doing? I'm typing. And no smart-ass remarks, please."

"I wasn't going to get smart," I said. "I was going to compliment you on your technique. You must be up to twenty-five, twenty-six words a minute now."

"Up your gazzo, too." She looked at her watch. "You're late."

"I'm the boss," I pointed out. "How'd you do on the research?"

"Well," McGraw said, pointing to a stack of folders on my desk. "I did well. Or as *you* might say, I did good."

"You're correcting me *before* I make the mistakes now?"

"Saves time," McGraw said.

"Any calls?" I asked.

McGraw nodded. "Four. One from Farns, who said, quote, 'Tell the kid I'm in place and ready.' One from Sam at O'Brien's who said your bar bill is getting outasight. One from Fat Freddie, your bookmaker, who said call him. And one from Diane Carter, who would like you to meet her for lunch at the Chenoweth House on Brownsboro Road." McGraw looked at her watch. "You would have been on time three minutes ago."

TEN

THE main dining room at Chenoweth House was spacious and bright, furnished with leafy ferns and small tables. Diane Carter was seated in the center of the room, surrounded by tables full of blue-haired ladies and business folk in suits and ties. She stood up when I approached and I couldn't help but notice that she was wearing a simple but expensive-looking dress that outlined her willowy figure. She grabbed my hand and shook it firmly.

"It's good to see you again, Michael."

"It's nice to see you."

We sat down and ordered drinks—I asked for a glass of white wine, she ordered vodka with a twist—and after the waitress delivered them, Diane said, "I came into town on some business and I finished a little earlier than I expected. So I decided to give you a call and see if you were free for lunch. I appreciate your meeting me on such short notice, Michael."

"What did you want to see me about?"

She smiled. "You certainly don't beat around the bush, do you?"

"Why beat around the bush?"

"Why indeed?" She picked up her drink, sipped it, set it down on the table. "I'm going to be frank with you, Michael. I need someone to talk to, someone to confide in. That's why I asked you to meet me here."

I nodded, not at all surprised. People were always

THE QUEEN'S MARE

confiding in me, telling me shit I didn't want to hear. Getting your ears beat was part of the private-eye job description. Listening to clients' stories came with the territory.

"I've only known you a short time, Michael, but I feel that I can trust you."

"The problem is not whether you can trust me," I said. "It's whether I can trust you. It's whether you can tell me the truth."

"What do you mean?"

"I mean in the business I'm in, the one thing you can count on is that everyone lies."

"Everyone?"

I nodded.

"Even clients?"

"*Especially* clients."

"But why? Why would a client lie to you?"

"That's not the right question. The right question is why wouldn't they?"

"But that's so... I don't know... cynical."

"Maybe so," I said, "but there it is."

"I have no reason to lie to you," Diane Carter said, "and I *do* feel that I can trust you. I hope I'm right about that."

"I hope you are, too," I said. "But who knows? It depends on what you want to trust me with, and what you mean by trust, and a half dozen other things. Trust doesn't come easy in my business."

"I guess I'm going about this all wrong," she said, and seemed genuinely contrite.

"No problem," I said. "Tell me what's bothering you"

"Well, for one thing I'm worried about Hattie," she said after a moment. "About her... ability to... I don't know... bear up in the face of things."

"She struck me as a very tough lady."

"She *is* tough," Diane Carter said, "but she is under great stress, great pressure... and between us, her health...is not...She has a problem...with her heart. You must not mention that to anyone. Very few people know of Hattie's heart condition. It's exacerbated by a lot of things. There have been some"—she hesitated—"personal things, family matters. Hattie and her grandchildren are not on the best of terms. She has some evidence that both Shirley and Charlotte might have joined forces with the stockholders who want to unseat her. She regards this naturally as a betrayal.

"But the greatest source of stress is the financial condition of the farm. To be quite frank, the farm has overextended itself in terms of loans. There is a significant cash-flow problem. Now on top of all that, Winterset has been kidnapped. I just don't know if she can handle it all."

She sipped at her drink. "And I'm not sure where telling you all this fits in. Except, I guess I needed some reassurance. I wanted to see you again and talk to you, make sure that you were the kind of tough competent character you seemed to be yesterday."

"I'm okay," I said. "I'm not the toughest guy on the block, but I'm in the top ten. I'm no knight on a white horse galloping in at the last minute to save everything, but I do all right. Most of the time I do what I set out to do."

"I guess that's what I wanted to hear," she said. "That you were someone who could deal with the thieves, handle what needed to be handled. Hattie so needs you to succeed in this, Michael—" She broke off as her eyes brimmed with tears.

I didn't know what else to do, so I reached across the table and patted her hand. "Take it easy, babe."

Diane Carter took a tissue out of her purse and dabbed at her eyes. "I'm sorry," she said, "forgive me. I don't usually get so emotional." She sniffled.

"Let's talk about something else," I said. "Let's talk about what you wanted to discuss yesterday—about who you think stole the mare and the foal."

Diane didn't seem surprised by my suggestion. She dabbed at her eyes, then put away the tissue. She said, "I think that might be a good idea, but I want to make it clear that I am only willing to talk about *my* feelings. I won't reveal anything about Hattie's suspicions, not without her permission. Is that understood, Michael?"

"Sure."

"And I think we ought to go ahead and have lunch first, don't you?"

"That's fine."

"Are you hungry, Michael?"

"I'm always hungry," I said. She laughed, as if I had made a joke. But it was the truth.

We ordered lunch then and over the food—soup and salad and sandwiches—made small talk, exchanging information about our backgrounds.

Diane told me she was from Lexington originally, the youngest daughter of a retired postal worker and a registered nurse. She had gone through the Lexington public school system, then on to UK, where she majored in communications and did some acting in student theater productions. She'd graduated with honors and had taken a job with a public relations firm in Louisville. Ten years ago she'd answered an ad for an entry-level position with Ashtree Farms and the rest was history, so to speak. Her official title now was director of operations, but she wore a dozen different hats and did everything from pitching in with the help to muck out the stalls to selling and promoting Ashtree's equine services on the international Thoroughbred market.

Operations director at Ashtree was a demanding, exciting job and she loved every minute of it. She was thirty-six years old, had no time for relationships or steady boyfriends, but every once in a while she managed to go out on a date. She was still interested and was still looking for something—the right man, the right relationship, but so far, had not been very lucky in that department. And over the years, and in the course of things, Hattie Beaumont and Diane Carter had grown extremely close to one another, and had become, in effect, pretty much like a mother and a daughter to each other. She felt, she said, like she was part of Hattie's family.

In turn I gave Diane a sketchy account of growing up in the West End of Louisville, dropping out of school early, joining the army, serving in Vietnam for eleven months, then returning home. I told her about working for the commonwealth attorney's office for a while as an investigator and attending college for a couple of years. I told her about drifting into the private-eye trade and discovering that I had a talent for it.

By this time we had finished eating and were lingering over a couple of after-lunch drinks. Diane lit a cigarette, took a sip of her drink, and said, "I'm ready to talk about the theft, but our conversation has to remain private. I don't want *anyone* to know that we talked about this. Agreed?"

I nodded.

"Yesterday I used the term 'list of suspects,'" she said, "but the truth is there are only two people on my list. One is Lucky Thompson."

"Lucky Thompson?" I repeated. "The trainer?"

Diane nodded. "He also happens to be one of the biggest minority stockholders in Ashtree Farms."

Lucky Thompson was one of the leading Thoroughbred horse trainers in America and by all odds the most famous. Horses he had trained had captured some of the biggest stakes races in the country, including the Derby and the other Triple Crown races. But Lucky's horses were not as well known as Lucky, who was the recipient of a good deal of favorable publicity, the subject of numerous magazine and newspaper articles. He appeared frequently on television, wearing five-hundred-dollar suits and affecting the demeanor of a wise old down-home Kentucky hardboot who also happened to be America's greatest horse trainer. Rumor had it that Lucky was an asshole and mean old bastard, but I had never met the man.

I recalled something about him, though. "Didn't he use to train for Ashtree?"

"Yes," Diane said. "Lucky was once head trainer of Ashtree. Until Hattie fired him."

"Tell me about that," I said.

Diane picked up her drink and took a long, deep swallow. She lit a fresh cigarette off an old one, blew out a big cloud of smoke, and started talking.

Five years ago this past November Hattie had discovered Lucky attempting to administer an unlawful substance, a form of a steroid, actually, to an Ashtree Farms colt. The country's top trainer notwithstanding, Hattie had fired him on the spot, and the state racing commission had brought him up on charges. There was no real evidence against Lucky other than Hattie's word and the commission had been unable to sustain the charges against him. Lucky had then brought suit against Ashtree for defamation of character. The court case dragged on for three years or more and finally, on the advice of Ashtree's attorney, Wallace Thornton, Hattie had settled the suit out of court.

That appeared to be the end of it except that one night shortly after the settlement Lucky Thompson showed up at Ashtree Farms and threatened revenge on Hattie. Diane had been present and had heard Thompson vow to get even with Hattie. He was drunk and profane and abusive, but Hattie Beaumont had not been afraid. She had laughed in his face and dismissed his threats as idle and impotent. Diane was not so sure. She had discovered that over the past few years Lucky had headed up a group of New York investors who had been purchasing large blocks of Ashtree stock; her latest information was that at the board meeting next week Lucky planned to mount a challenge to Hattie's authority.

"I heard him that night on the farm," she said. "I heard him say that no matter how long it took he would get back at Hattie, make her sorry for what he said she had done to him." Diane stabbed her cigarette out in the ashtray. "It wouldn't surprise me at all to find out that Thompson had engineered the kidnapping as a way of striking back at Hattie."

"But you don't have any evidence of this, do you?"

"No, I'm afraid not. It's all just my idea of how it all could have happened," Diane said.

She was right. It was nothing but speculation and conjecture. On the other hand, if she was accurate about Lucky, he had means, motive, and opportunity. Lucky had been in Kentucky all spring, since the beginning of the Keeneland meet, and was not due to leave until the Downs meet ended next month.

"Who's your other suspect?" I asked.

ELEVEN

I signaled the waitress for two more drinks while Diane lighted a fresh cigarette. I waited until after the waitress had served us before I repeated my question.

"Your other suspect?"

She hesitated, her eyes on mine, then said, "Shirley Beaumont."

"Charlotte's sister? Hattie's other granddaughter?"

"Yes."

"What makes you suspect her?"

"I don't know that *suspect* is the right word. I just think that Shirley is capable of something as extreme as the kidnapping. She's a very bitter, ambitious woman. She wants to take over the reins of power at Ashtree. She sees herself as a kind of super-businesswoman. She's director of the Kentucky Association of Businesswomen, which is a rather strange organization full of lesbians and militant feminists. Shirley herself is a lesbian, and while I don't mean that I think that is the reason she is capable of doing something so extreme, it does put her in with some rather unsavory elements. She is part owner of a new nightclub in the West End, a place that caters to drug users. It's called Greenstreets."

I'm slow, and sometimes you have to pound something into my head, but I caught that one immediately. The connection between Curtis Graves and Ashtree Farms became suddenly clearer.

"I hate to ruin the party all the time," I said, "but what about any evidence of Shirley's involvement in the kidnapping?"

Diane shook her head. "Nothing. I may be mistaken about Shirley. The fact is, except for wanting to take over, she doesn't show much interest in the farm. Shirley seldom comes out there. She has a house in old Louisville and spends most of her time there and in her office in the Starks Building."

Diane sighed. "The truth is, that neither of Hattie's granddaughters come out to see her as often as they should. Charlotte is out of town most of the time but even when she's in Louisville, she stays away from the farm. I asked her why once and she said that the place holds bad memories for her because of the accident. It happened out in front of the farm, you know. On the highway in front of the main entrance."

Hattie Beaumont had mentioned an accident involving her son, and Charlotte's phrase about attributing her grandmother's decline to the accident came back to me. "Is this the accident that killed Mrs. Beaumont's son?" I asked.

Diane looked surprised. "You don't know about the accident?"

I shook my head. "I don't think so."

She laughed. "That shows you how you can lose perspective. The accident has such a significance to the Beaumonts and played so big a role in the family history that I think those of us in the family and close to it just assume that everyone knows about it. While the truth is that most people don't know anything about it."

She took a small sip of her drink. "It happened in 1964, April the first of 1964. It was a terrible, tragic thing. It is the Beaumont family's great tragedy. Four people were killed. Hattie's son James and his wife and the Hacketts."

"The Hacketts?"

Diane nodded. "Meg's parents. Her father was an

assistant trainer at Ashtree then. He and his wife were in the car with James Beaumont and *his* wife, whose name was Evelyn, I believe. James Beaumont was driving and I think there was liquor involved. At any rate, he pulled out of the main entrance onto the highway right into the path of an oncoming car. They were all killed. Instantly, I understand." She put her cigarette out in the ashtray.

"Six children were orphaned by the accident. Charlotte and Shirley and the Hackett children. Besides Meg, there were two brothers and a sister, I think. They went to live with relatives, I believe. Shirley and Charlotte were about ten years old. They stayed at Ashtree with their grandparents. Hattie's husband died the following year, and Hattie brought the children up by herself essentially." Diane picked up her glass and set it back down without drinking from it.

"How Meg came to work for the same family her father once worked for is quite simple. Five years ago Hattie advertised for a housekeeper–companion and Meg showed up at the door and asked for the job. Hattie remembered her, of course, and took her in and she's been with us all this time and is just like a member of the family now."

She looked at me. "It's quite a story, isn't it? I mean the way something like an accident can affect people's lives so drastically." She picked up her glass and took a drink this time. Then she looked at me again. "Is anything wrong?"

"Wrong?"

"It's just that you were staring off into space."

"I was just thinking about something," I said.

Diane took a compact mirror out of her purse and studied herself in it. "I'm glad I told you about my suspicions, Michael. Maybe I'm wrong. I hope I am about Shirley. But I'm glad I told you about them. Perhaps they'll be helpful." She looked at her watch. "I'm going to have to run. I've got to meet the caterer at two. I'm in charge of the party arrangements."

"Party?"

She nodded. "Tonight's the annual stockholders' party. It's held every year at Ashtree, and we're going on with it just as if nothing is wrong."

I nodded, my feelings unhurt by not being invited. The only invitations private eyes received were to close-out sales and grand openings. "I just have a couple more questions," I said. "Ashtree's equine insurance. Who handles it?"

"Why do you want to know that?"

"The more things I know," I said, "the better I can do my job."

"His name is John Dixon. He has an office on Hurtsbourne Lane."

"My other question," I said, "is not really a question. It's a kind of warning. I'm not positive that Eddie Walker was involved in the kidnapping, but I've got a feeling that he knows more than he's saying. I want you and Mrs. Beaumont to be aware of that."

"I'll relay your message to Hattie." She returned the mirror to her purse. Then she leaned across the table and took my hands in hers. "I want to thank you, Michael. I feel so much better after talking to you. I'm not as worried about the outcome, *whoever* took the horses. I really believe that you're going to do whatever it takes to make this thing come out all right."

She took a card out of her purse and handed it to me. It had her name and her job title and a phone number on it. "That's my private number," she said. "Call me when you want to. Perhaps, when all this is over . . ."

She looked at me. It was a look full of promise. She glanced at her watch, said, "Oh God, I've got to go," and stood up. "Call me soon," she said, and turned and strode off. I watched her walk across the room to the exit.

I picked up my glass and took a sip of wine. It was

dry and tart but it had lost its chill. There wasn't any use in thinking about accidents or the past. That led you nowhere. I needed to think about the things Diane Carter had told me. So I made myself think about the broodmare and her foal and the thieves and Hattie Beaumont and Lucky Thompson and Curtis Graves and Shirley Beaumont and Ashtree Farms and the Queen of England, who was coming in five days. And I thought about the million dollars in ransom.

It's a good thing, I said to myself, that you can't tell anyone about this, because if you could no one would believe you anyway. In some strange way that notion made me feel better. I put some money down on the table and stood up. Lunch was over. It was time to go back to work.

TWELVE

WHEN I got back to the office McGraw was gone. She had left a note on her desk: *Linguistics switched to Wednesday at 2. Martial Arts at 6. Lunch at three. Back at 4.* The note referred to McGraw's schedule, and like McGraw it was not easy to understand.

I took off my sport coat, draped it over the chair, sat down at my desk, and began to sift through the research material that McGraw had compiled. There were three folders. The two thickest ones contained material—newspaper clippings, photographs, articles, and items—on Ashtree Farms, Hattie Beaumont, and the Beaumont family. I spent some time going through them and learned that Hattie was seventy-one years old, had been a widow for the past twenty-some years, and was celebrated in the racing industry for her many contributions to the sport.

The articles about the farm were concerned mostly with the numerous Thoroughbreds that had raced under the Beaumont colors. These included some of the most famous names in racing over the past three decades. There was a copy of the newspaper coverage of the accident that had killed Hattie's son. It showed pictures of the four victims. You could see something of the old woman in the son's eyes and nose. There was also some material on Lucky Thompson, including an article about his suit against Ashtree. Substantially, it confirmed Diane Carter's version of events.

There was a fair amount of material on Hattie's granddaughters, including pictures of both women at different ages. From her newspaper photographs, Shirley appeared to be a trim, tanned blond with a beautiful smile. A professional tennis player who once played a quarter final match at Wimbledon, she had retired from the game at the age of thirty-two, returned to Louisville, and founded the Kentucky Association of Businesswomen. The association was a nonprofit organization that lobbied for the rights of local businesswomen. The articles characterized the organization as "controversial," but none of them said anything about lesbians.

Charlotte's photographs were mostly publicity handouts, but in one shot that showed her as a young woman the resemblance to Paige was remarkable. Most of the written material on her was in the form of reviews of her roles in the different plays she had appeared in, but some of it had to do with her personal life. She had been married several times and had made a few headlines. There were tabloid accounts of her marital problems and an article that dealt with her rehabilitation from, as the piece put it, "a drug and alcohol related problem." Charlotte had appeared in several Hollywood films and in a number of Broadway shows, and while she seemed to work pretty steadily as a professional actress, she had never, apparently, become a star or a famous name.

The other folder contained material on Wallace Thornton and articles from the business pages about Ashtree Farms's financial problems. The stuff on Thornton was boring. University of Kentucky. Harvard Law School. His association with several different firms. His expertise on equine property law. His position as chief legal counsel for Ashtree Farms.

The business articles about Ashtree on the other hand made for some interesting reading. They dealt with some of the matters that Diane Carter had mentioned, insufficient cash flow, overextension on a number of loans—but the one that grabbed my attention concerned an unspecified group of investors who were trying to force the farm into involuntary bankruptcy. This group owned 3.8 million in Ashtree bonds and intended to sue the farm for the unpaid interest on the bonds and a substantial amount of money for damages. I was reading the part that described why as secured creditors they would be the first to be paid when the office phone rang.

I picked up the receiver. "Rhineheart Investigations."

"Peeper." The gravelly voice of Detective Sergeant Sidney Katz, Louisville police department, rumbled over the wire. Katz was an old... *Friend* wasn't the right word. Neither was *enemy*. *Antagonist*, maybe. I'm not sure there's a word that properly covers our relationship. Katz and I have bumped heads more than a few times over the course of the years.

"What can I do for you, Katz?"

"Come over and see me, Peeper."

"I'm busy, Katz."

"See can you get unbusy," Katz said. "I got someone here wants to talk to you."

"Who?"

"His name's Dixon. He's with the State, so to speak."

"What's this in regard to, Katz?"

"In regard, old friend, to cooperating in an investigation concerning the theft and possible ransom of a valuable broodmare and her foal."

"I'll be over in a few minutes, Katz."

"We're looking forward to it, Peep."

I put down the phone, picked it right back up, and dialed the number of Ashtree Farms. Meg Hackett answered the phone. I identified myself and told her I wanted to speak to Mrs. Beaumont.

After a minute Hattie Beaumont came on the line. "What's wrong, Mr. Rhineheart?"

THE QUEEN'S MARE 71

"Louisville police just called. They want to talk to me about the ransom of a broodmare."

"Oh my," Hattie Beaumont said. "How do you suppose they found out?"

"Good question."

"You think someone here at the farm told them?"

"No idea. I called to tell you that if you have any strings, now is the time to pull them."

"I'll do what I can," she said. "What are you going to tell them?"

"As little as I can," I said. "I'm going to stonewall."

"Are you good at that, Mr. Rhineheart?"

"On a scale of ten, I'm a twelve."

"Good luck" was the last thing Mrs. Beaumont said.

Katz's box-sided little office on the third floor of police headquarters was crowded. Besides Katz, who was wearing his usual scowl and a tan suit that looked like it came off the rack at K-Mart, there was a black guy with steel-rimmed glasses and a neatly trimmed Afro, a young bearded guy in a uniform—navy blazer, khaki-colored duck pants, cordovan penny loafers, blue shirt with a button-down collar, and a red-and-white striped tie—and a stenographer who sported oversized designer rims, a mane of luxurious dark hair, and a short skirt that revealed a pair of shapely legs.

The black guy, I figured, was Dixon, the state cop. The bearded, penny-loafer wearer was either an assistant D.A. or on the Commonwealth Attorney's staff. The stenographer wore a name tag that identified her as Debbie Dawson.

"Why," I said, "does this place remind me of *A Night at the Opera*?"

Katz didn't respond, nor did he bother to introduce me to anyone. He grimaced, pointed to an empty chair, and said, "You want us to read you your rights now, Peeper, or wait until later?"

THIRTEEN

I flopped down in the chair. "Gee," I addressed the Commonwealth's Attorney guy, "this sounds awfully serious."

He nodded somberly. "It *is* serious."

"Am I being arrested for something?" I asked the black guy. The black guy looked at Katz, who said, "Not necessarily, Rhineheart. Not if you come up with the right answers to our questions."

"I think I want my lawyer present," I said. My lawyer's an Irish gambler named Brendan Flynn, who spends more time at the racetrack than he does in court. While that's some measure of his legal ability, it is not as revealing as the fact that Brendan owes *me* money.

Katz snatched up the phone and held it out toward me. "Go ahead." Katz knew that on a weekday afternoon in May Flynn would be sitting in the clubhouse at Churchill Downs.

"On the other hand," I said, "maybe you better go ahead and read me my rights."

Katz stuck a Camel between his lips, lighted it, coughed, sucked in a lungful of smoke, coughed again, spit a stream of smoke in my direction, and said, "That can wait till later."

In an impatient voice, the black guy said, "Sergeant Katz, let's cut out all the bullshitting and bluffing and tell the man why he's here."

THE QUEEN'S MARE 73

Katz looked surprised, then he shrugged, and said, "It's your party, Dix. Proceed."

Dixon spoke to me. "I'm Walker Dixon, special investigator for the Kentucky State Police. This here," he jerked a thumb at the bearded guy, "is Tom Washburn. Tom's an assistant prosecutor with the State Attorney General's office. Sergeant Katz has been kind enough to act as local liaison for us in contacting you, Rhineheart."

"What's Debbie doing here?" I asked.

The stenographer blushed, looked down at her name tag, covered it for a moment with her hand, looked even more embarrassed, then put her hand back in her lap, and began to squirm in her chair.

Washburn spoke up. "We thought it might be advantageous to have a record of the proceedings." At a look from Dixon, he cleared his throat and said, "We were probably mistaken about that. I have no objection to removing the stenographer, if the rest of us are in agreement on that."

Dixon looked at Katz.

Katz spread his hands. "It's okay by me." He raised both eyebrows. "Debbie, would you mind? I'll call you later if we need you."

I smiled at Debbie to show her there were no hard feelings. She blushed again, rose awkwardly out of her chair, and hurried out of the room.

"Let's get down to business," Dixon said. He whipped off the steel rims and pinched the bridge of his nose. "Rhineheart, we're in possession of all the pertinent information. From the theft of the broodmare and her foal two nights ago to your meeting with Wallace Thornton at Professional Towers yesterday afternoon, including everything in between, like the ransom demand and your talk with Mrs. Beaumont and her assistant. We got all the facts and the figures. Winterset and her foal, a male horse sired by the stallion, BuckMaster. Both of them owned by the Queen of

England. One million dollars in ransom in used one-hundred-dollar bills. We know everything. We even know that the thieves mentioned your name in their initial call. Why do you think they did that, Rhineheart?"

I said nothing.

"That's all right," Dixon said. "You don't have to answer. It doesn't matter. We don't think the name dropping was significant. I'm not sure you give a shit, but if it means anything, you're not a suspect, Rhineheart. I'm telling you that out front so you'll know we're being straight with you."

He paused a moment, put his glasses back on, and jabbed a finger at me. "What we want from you is simple. Confirmation of some facts and a little cooperation."

"What kind of cooperation?" I asked.

"Permission to put a tap on your phone. Participation in a project we have relative to the ransom exchange."

"Tell me about this project," I said.

"No big deal," Washburn said. "We set up a trap for the thieves. You'll wear a wire. We'll come down on the scene at the appropriate time. That way your client doesn't lose a thing. She gets her horses back *and* her money. We get the thieves red-handed and on the wire, and everybody lives happily after."

"Plus," I said, "you get a lot of ink for capturing some horsenappers. It might even make the wire services."

"Absolutely nothing wrong with favorable publicity," Washburn said. "Most large city departments even have their own P.R. units."

I nodded. "The whole thing sounds very nice," I said. "The only thing is I don't know what the fuck you all are talking about. If I had such a client with the kind of problem that you're describing, I'd be obligated to keep it to myself. It'd be unethical for me to discuss it with you guys."

Washburn looked startled, as if someone had just spit in his face. Katz, on the other hand, smiled and wagged a finger at Dixon. "I told you, Dix. I told you what the fucker was like."

Dixon's face contorted in rage. "You sonofabitch," he erupted, "you think you can play fuck-around with us, you got another goddamn think coming. Katz, read this asshole his rights. We're going to take him down to the interrogation room and tear his fucking head off."

Katz had a strange look on his face. Half smile, half grimace, as if he was enjoying himself for getting fucked over. He asked Dixon what they were going to charge me with.

"Charge him with any fucking thing," Dixon said. "I don't care. Suspicion, withholding information, conspiracy, any goddamn thing'll do."

"Conspiracy?" Washburn's tone was questioning. "Lieutenant—" he started.

"Katz," Dixon said, "read the man his rights."

Katz heaved a big sigh.

"Never mind," Dixon snapped. "I'll do it myself." He addressed me. "You got the right to remain silent, motherfucker. You got the right—"

The phone at Katz's elbow buzzed. He snatched it up, listened for a moment, then held it out to Dixon.

"Tell whoever it is—"

"It's your chief," Katz said.

Dixon, whose chest was heaving, took a moment to compose himself, then accepted the phone from Katz. Washburn said something to me, but I wasn't listening. I was studying Dixon's face. It reminded me of the face of a recruit I had once seen who was getting his ass chewed out by a master sergeant.

Dixon began to nod. He said yessir three times, nosir once, then yessir three more times before he handed the phone back to Katz. Without a look in my direction, he spun on his heel and stomped out of the office. Katz and Washburn exchanged a look. They got up and followed Dixon into the hall.

A few minutes later Katz returned, alone. "What's going on here, Rhineheart? The state police *chief* calls up and tells Dixon to go easy on you. All of a sudden you got *influence*? A lowlife, half-ass gumshoe like yourself?"

I stood up. "Am I free to leave?"

Katz nodded. "But remember one thing."

"What's that, Katz?"

"Mrs. Beaumont ain't gonna be your client forever, you know."

"That a threat?" I asked.

Katz nodded. "Yeah."

FOURTEEN

My car was right where I had left it—in a LOADING ZONE ONLY spot down the block from the office. There was a parking ticket stuck behind the wiper on the driver's side. I took it off the window and threw it in the backseat with the others.

I drove out River Road to a restaurant called the Captain's Quarters. Seated outdoors, on a deck overlooking the Ohio River, I ate clams and oysters, drank two glasses of white wine, and kidded with the waitress whose name was Sherrie, and who seemed to be an admirable person in many respects, not the least of which were her svelte body and her oval-shaped face with its smattering of freckles. After dinner I drove home.

The first thing I did was check with my answering service. There were four messages from Dan Horner asking me to please get back in touch with him. I put my weapon away and hung the holster on the closet door. I threw on jeans and a sweater, put on a pair of beat-up Wallabies, and went for a walk around the neighborhood. I was living, that year, in the Highlands section of Louisville. It was a quiet, respectable area of nice homes and broad streets and well-kept lawns. My neighbors were shopkeepers and legal secretaries and university teachers. *I* was probably the most unsavory character in the neighborhood. I walked for twenty-five minutes, enjoying the cool, evening air and the quiet streets. By the time I got back to my place, darkness had fallen. I switched on the front-room lamp and picked up the telephone, which was ringing. Hattie Beaumont was on the line and her voice sounded tense.

"Mr. Rhineheart, I just received a call from the thieves. I informed them of our arrangement. They want to talk directly to you. They're going to call back in two hours."

In the background behind Hattie's voice I could hear the sound of music and chatter. Tonight, as Diane had mentioned, was the night of the annual stockholders' party.

"I'll be there in forty minutes," I said, and had a sudden thought. "I'm going to bring someone with me," I added. "A date."

"Fine." Hattie Beaumont's voice sounded doubtful. As soon as the connection was broken, I dialed McGraw. "Put on your high-heeled sneakers," I told her. "We're going to a party at Ashtree Farms."

"*Tonight?*"

"I'll pick you up in twenty minutes."

"Oh God," McGraw wailed, "I don't have anything to wear."

"Put *something* on, babe. Be out in front of your place." I hung up, struggled into a suit and tie, clipped on a belt holster, and got my "party gun," a snub nose .32, out of the closet. Too small to make a noticeable bulge, the .32 was a reliable weapon if trouble developed.

I picked McGraw up in front of her apartment. She was wearing a simple off-white dress and a gold chain around her neck. She began talking the minute she got in the car and kept up a line of nervous chatter all the way to Ashtree.

"Can I come along when you go on the ransom thing?"

"It's called an exchange."

"Can I go along on the exchange?"

"Don't be silly."

"I've never been on a ransom exchange before."

"What do you mean, you've never been on a ransom exchange before? Who the fuck has? You think it's some kind of *common* experience?"

"Don't get mad at me," McGraw said. "And don't swear. '*You* have' is the answer to your question. If I remember correctly, you went on a ransom drop last year. The Underwood case. You get to have all the fun."

"Fun?"

"And you know *why*, Rhineheart? You know why you get to go on all the ransom drops and exchanges?"

"Because I'm the detective?"

"No. That's not the reason."

"It's not?"

"No," McGraw said. "You want me to tell you why you get to do all the important stuff?"

"No," I said, "I'd rather you didn't."

"Well, I'm going to tell you anyway."

I said, "Yeah, I figured you might."

"It's because you're a man," McGraw said. "That's why you get to do all the meaningful stuff. Men go on the ransom exchanges, while women sit around and worry about them."

There it was: the feminist perspective on ransom drops.

"McGraw," I said, "I'd love to talk to you more about this, but I got to concentrate on the driving."

"That's okay," she said. "You don't have to talk. Just keep your eyes on the road and listen."

The party was going full blast when we arrived. The downstairs rooms were filled with well-dressed people, standing about, drinks in hand, chatting. In one room there was a piano and a piano player, and couples danced in a small cleared-off space. The adjoining room contained lines of tables loaded down with food and drink. Waiters, in short white coats, passed from room to room, carrying trays of drinks.

Diane Carter came over and introduced herself to McGraw. While they talked I looked around for Charlotte Beaumont, but she was not in sight.

"Eddie Walker didn't show up for work today," Diane said to me. "When I called his apartment no one answered. You must be right about him."

I nodded glumly. Being right about shit, I had discovered a long time ago, was no big deal.

"Lucky Thompson is here," Diane said. She nodded her head in the direction of a man on the other side of the room. A short fellow in evening jacket and black tie, he was standing next to a tall young woman who from all the way across the room had the unmistakable look of a high-priced hooker.

"How come he's so short?" McGraw asked.

I looked at her. Four-eleven in her stocking feet and she was wondering why someone was short. "He used to be a jockey," I said.

Diane Carter asked McGraw if she would like to meet Hattie Beaumont. McGraw nodded and said, "Yes, anything to get away from these bad looks Rhineheart is giving me." They wandered off and I stood there holding a drink and listening to the piano player, who wasn't Art Tatum, but who wasn't bad.

"Are you Mr. Rhineheart?"

I turned to find a slim, attractive woman that I recognized from her pictures as Shirley Beaumont standing in front of me. "Hello," I said.

"It's a pleasure to meet you." Her voice was neutral, accentless. Her years on the pro tennis circuit had apparently bleached out all trace of Kentucky. She had cool blue eyes and neat symmetrical features. She wore her hair in bangs that feathered over her forehead. She was holding a tall glass of what looked like Scotch.

"It's all right," I said.

"Your, uh, associate, seems to be enjoying herself."

I glanced over at McGraw, who was standing with a group of people that included Hattie Beaumont and Diane Carter. McGraw had a wineglass in one hand and seemed to be doing okay, chatting away with Mrs. Beaumont, holding her own conversationally with the other guests. I hadn't heard any *motherfuckers* or *sonsofbitches* coming from McGraw's direction, and I was grateful for that.

"McGraw likes to party," I said.

"Grandmother seems to have taken her under her wing," she observed, and something in her tone made me look at her and say, "You don't approve?"

"It isn't a question of whether or not I approve, Mr. Rhineheart. Grandmother has a penchant for taking strangers under her wing. It's one of her character traits. She's closer to her operations director than she is to her own blood."

"Your sister calls Mrs. Beaumont 'Mother,'" I said. "I notice that you don't."

She uttered a brittle little laugh. "Charlotte is a confused person, Mr. Rhineheart. She has problems with boundaries and relations. As does her daughter. One of the problems with this family, Mr. Rhineheart, is that the people in it don't know their true relationship to one another."

She finished off her drink and plucked another from the tray of a passing waiter. She took a hit off it, then resumed the conversation. "But I don't want you to misunderstand me, Mr. Rhineheart. I'm not being critical of Grandmother. I admire her a great deal. In many respects, she's a remarkable woman. Grandfather died shortly after my father's death, and Grandmother took over the reins of the family enterprises. Until quite recently she has been very successful. She has an outstanding reputation in the Thoroughbred industry. I hope to do half as well when my turn comes."

It was time to play the straight man. "Your turn?"

"I am executive vice president of Ashtree, Mr.

Rhineheart. Organizationally, second in command. I've been in the family business for some time now, even while I was pursuing other goals. I own several small related businesses myself," she added.

And one nonrelated one. I considered asking her about Greenstreets, then decided against it. No use throwing cards on the table in advance.

"I recently completed my M.B.A.," she continued, "and I have an M.S. in finance and business development." She stretched her mouth modestly. "I have become something of an expert in capital investment as it relates to the equine industry. I expect to succeed to the presidency of Ashtree when Grandmother retires."

I was about to ask her if she thought her grandmother's retirement was an imminent prospect when she added, "Incidentially, Mr. Rhineheart, I was and am in full support of Grandmother's decision not to inform the authorities and to use you as a go-between in the ransom exchange. Not everyone in the family agrees with Grandmother about this, but I am behind her one hundred percent. Given the situation and the limited amount of alternatives, I feel it's a reasonable way to proceed. One can only hope that the ransom exchange goes smoothly and successfully."

My way of responding to this was to take a sip of my drink—bourbon and water—and wonder what Shirley Beaumont's support meant. How much voting stock did she own? Her title was executive vice president, but was that nominal or did she wield some real power? *Not everyone in the family* put Charlotte in the position of outsider.

"I understand there's something of a cash-flow problem," Shirley Beaumont said. "Do you happen to know if Wallace has had any trouble putting together the ransom sum?"

I smiled politely and took another sip of my drink.

"You're not exactly a mountain of information, are you, Mr. Rhineheart?" Shirley Beaumont said this with

THE QUEEN'S MARE 83

a smile on her face, but when she glanced past me, the smile disappeared and a small line appeared between her eyebrows. "Ah," she said, "here's my lovely sister, the not-very-famous actress." Her voice was shooting for a light bantering tone, but missing badly. Behind the breezy delivery, you could hear a lot of bitterness and scorn.

I turned around in time to see Charlotte, who was accompanied by a dour-looking Wallace Thornton, give her sister a steely-eyed look, say, "Save the bullshit, Shirley," in a peremptory voice, then turn her face in my direction and bestow a dazzling smile on me. "Mr. Rhineheart, my very favorite private-eye person. How are you this evening? Well, I hope."

"I'm all right," I said. "You look . . ." She was wearing a low-cut silk dress and no bra. The tips of her nipples pressed against the fabric. Her breasts . . . I gave up searching for the right word. "Good" was all I could come up with.

She gave me a slight nod, as if that was all the compliment deserved. "Tell me, has Shirley been boring you to death with her capital investment in the equine industry routine, or has she been trying to get you to attend one of her weird parties?" Charlotte turned and addressed her sister. "You're wasting your time, sweetie. I wouldn't think Mr. Rhineheart would go for those AC–DC affairs you throw, although"—she raised an eyebrow my way—"you never really know, do you? Maybe he likes that sort of stuff." She moved past me and held out her arms. "How are you, Shirley? You may kiss me, only watch you don't mess with my makeup."

"Thanks, but I'll pass," Shirley Beaumont said and took a swallow of her drink instead.

"It's just as well," Charlotte said. She turned back to me and under her breath but loud enough to be heard she said, "With Shirley's sexual habits, there's no telling what sort of disease she may be transmitting these days."

"Your tits are hanging out of your dress, Charlotte," Shirley said, all the politeness gone from her voice.

"At least I have tits," Charlotte said, "and I know what they're for, sister."

"Still the big-mouthed, nasty bitch," Shirley Beaumont said in a loud voice that turned a few heads. Her face was pale and she looked at her sister with hatred. She stared at Charlotte a second longer and then turned quickly and strode away, out of the room.

"Forgive my sister, Mr. Rhineheart, for being such an unpleasant person." She turned to Thornton. "Wallace, be a gem and go fetch me a large vodka and tonic. And take your time. I want to talk to Mr. Rhineheart privately."

Thornton's somber look deepened, as if it might become a permanent part of his features. "Charlotte, you test a gentleman's patience."

"Yes," Charlotte agreed, "I do. That's true." Her eyes glittered. "But just think of the possible rewards, Wallace."

Thornton turned to me. "Can I get you anything from the bar, Mr. Rhineheart?"

"No thanks, Counselor."

Thornton looked as if he was about to say something, but he turned and walked away.

Charlotte giggled. "Wallace hates it when you say 'Counselor' like that. Did you see his face?"

"You were pretty hard on your sister. How come?"

Charlotte raised an eyebrow. It seemed to shock her that anyone might say something critical of her behavior. She smiled, but I could tell she was instantly displeased with me. "Shirley and I happen to dislike each other intensely, Mr. Rhineheart, not that it's any of your gawdamn snooping business." The smile had turned icy.

THE QUEEN'S MARE

I looked into her dark eyes. "What did you want to talk to me privately about?"

"Oh, I've changed my mind about that," she said. "I don't think I want to talk to you privately after all."

"Fine."

"Are you always this difficult?" Her tone was angry.

"Yeah," I said. "What about you?"

She looked at me and burst into laughter. "Yes," she said. "Actually, I'm worse than this." She reached out for my drink. "May I?"

"Knock yourself out," I said, handing her the glass.

She eyed the bourbon and water and ice. "What's in here?"

I told her. She took a long slow drink, then handed it back to me. "Let's dance," she said, and walked out into the cleared space, which was empty. I set the glass down on a table and followed her. The piano player began to play "I Can't Get Started," the old Bunny Berrigan tune. I took Charlotte in my arms. She was as light as air.

She looked into my eyes. "You want to take me home from here, Mr. Rhineheart?"

"I thought you were with Thornton."

"I'm not *with* anyone. People are *with* me. Wallace gave me a *lift* here. I come and go as I please."

"I'd love you take you home, but I'm here on business."

"And you never mix business with pleasure?"

"You're testing my principles, Ms. Beaumont."

"Call me 'Charlotte.'"

"You're testing my principles, Charlotte."

"I didn't think private eyes had principles."

"Just a few," I said. "One of them is doing what you hired on to do."

She snuggled closer. "What exactly is going on tonight, Mr. Rhineheart. Why are you here?"

I shrugged and smiled.

"I've been rejected," she said dramatically. "Don't

think I haven't encountered rejection in my career, Mr. Rhineheart. And in my personal and private life as well. I must say, however, that I don't believe I've ever been rejected for such lofty reasons before."

"And by a private eye to boot," I said. Then I added, "Actually, I find it hard to believe that you've ever been rejected by anyone for any reason."

"Do you?" She smiled, and if it wasn't quite dazzling, it was close. "Maybe I'll give you a second chance sometime. Thank you for the dance," she said. I let go of her and she turned and walked across the room.

I stood watching her until something hard slammed against my side. I turned and there was McGraw next to my elbow. She gave me a look. "What the fuck is the matter with you?" she said. "I said your name three times and hit you twice. An actress type dances with you and you stand around acting like Dopey Duck."

"What do you want?" I asked in an irritated voice.

"The thieves just called," she said. "They want to talk to you."

FIFTEEN

In the library Hattie Beaumont, Wallace Thornton, and Diane Carter were grouped around a table, where a telephone machine sat, its red light blinking. They were facing the door, waiting for me, and when McGraw and I entered the room they looked relieved. On a couch on the other side of the room, Meg Hackett sat bent over her sewing basket. She did not even look up.

As I crossed over to the phone I noticed a suitcase sitting on the floor next to the table. It didn't look big enough to hold a million dollars. It was an ordinary brown leather suitcase. Surely not, I thought. No one spoke as I walked up to the table, picked up the receiver, and depressed the hold button.

"This is Rhineheart."

"Listen up, Rhineheart." A man's voice. Country. Nasal. The age difficult to tell. Not an old man's voice, but not a kid either. "We spoke to the old lady. She told us you were gonna handle all the arrangements. That's fine with us so long as you keep your mouth shut, follow instructions, and don't do anything stupid. You understand what I'm saying?"

"You're coming through loud and clear," I said.

"You in possession of the money?"

I looked at Thornton, then down at the suitcase. He nodded.

"I'm in possession."

"Take it home with you. We'll call you there. Maybe later tonight. Maybe tomorrow."

"Wait," I said.

The phone went dead.

I put the receiver back on the machine. I turned to Hattie Beaumont. I told her what the thief had said. As I listened to myself speaking, it was pretty clear from my voice that I wasn't exactly thrilled at the prospect of transporting that much money in the Maverick back to my apartment.

"If he wants you to take it back to Louisville," Hattie Beaumont said, "then I suppose we'd best follow his instructions, don't you think?"

A shrug was the best I could do. I turned to Thornton. "What about you, Counselor? You got an opinion on this?"

"Do we have any other alternatives?"

"I don't think so," I said.

"Then we'd better do what he wants." Thornton reached down and picked up the suitcase. He set it flat on the table, inserted a key, and unlocked it. He pulled back the lid, revealing rows of tightly packed one-hundred-dollar bills. I looked at it and took a deep breath. Then I looked over at McGraw, who was standing there with her mouth open.

"You'll need to count it in front of witnesses," Thornton said, handing me the suitcase key. "To make sure it's all there."

"Is that necessary?" I said.

"I insist upon it," Thornton said. Money brought out the rock in the man.

"Perhaps you'd better," Mrs. Beaumont said.

"You want to help me?" I said to McGraw. Together, we counted the money. It took us thirty-five minutes. It was all there. We bundled it back into the suitcase, locked it, and I picked it up and hefted it. It was fairly heavy.

Hattie, Thornton, and Diane accompanied us as far

as the front porch. There were some guests in the drive. The headlights of a car came on. I stood there awkwardly hanging on to the suitcase, then set it down on the porch for a moment, then picked it right back up when a pair of partygoers appeared on the porch. From inside you could hear the tinkle of the piano. The party was still going strong.

Hattie Beaumont spoke: "Be careful, Mr. Rhineheart."

"Good luck," Thornton said.

I winced. The words sent a chill up my spine. They sounded like the wrong thing to say, a bad omen even, and they produced a vague, ominous feeling in me.

I drove, McGraw rode shotgun, and the suitcase sat between us on the drive back to Louisville. I let McGraw off in front of her place and drove over to my apartment. Suitcase in my left hand, Python in my right, I carried it inside and set it on the coffee table. Then I locked and bolted the door and pulled down the blinds.

I hung up my coat, laid the Python on the coffee table next to the suitcase, and sat down on the end of the couch closest to the front-room phone. I was still wearing my shoulder rig. Its brown leather went well with my tan button-down shirt. It was 10:36 P.M. There was a clean ashtray on the coffee table and it made me think about cigarettes. If I hadn't quit, I could smoke five or six in the next ten minutes and maybe that would help settle me down. I looked at my watch: 10:37. I was behaving like a real pro. At this rate, I'd go crazy by midnight. I told myself to be cool and relax. The call could come anytime. Maybe even tomorrow. Or the next day. Jesus Christ, I hoped not.

I picked up a book, a paperback collection of short stories, and stretched out on the couch with a cushion under my head. I shifted around a little until the shoulder holster strap stopped cutting into my shoulder. It was quiet in the apartment. If you listened closely you could hear the hum of the refrigerator in the kitchen.

I read the first sentence of the first story, "When he woke in the morning, his mind was filled with an image of the girl's face," and the telephone rang, startling me upright, the book spilling to the floor. I snatched up the receiver.

"Hello?"

"Rhineheart."

It was McGraw.

"I just called to see if you got home okay," she said.

I kept my voice level. "I'm fine, but McGraw, I don't think it's a good idea to call and tie up the line."

"Where's the money?"

"On the coffee table."

"How does it feel to be sitting there with a million bucks on your coffee table?"

"Not too great. You know what else feels bad? The idea of tying up this line when the thieves might be calling."

"Is that a hint for me to hang up?"

"It's no hint. Hang up, McGraw."

"I'll call you tomorrow," she said and hung up. I got up and went into the kitchen. There was a six-pack of beer in the refrigerator and some milk and packages of lunch meat and cheese. I fixed myself a bologna-and-cheese sandwich and spread some Miracle Whip on it. All the stuff had come out of plastic packages but it was pretty good. If someone had been looking in the window they would have seen a guy wearing an empty shoulder holster sitting at his kitchen table eating a sandwich.

I had a glass of milk and two Oreo cookies for dessert and wondered what a registered dietitian would think of my meal. Probably not much. I washed out my sandwich plate and my glass in the sink and wandered back into the front room. The suitcase sat there on the coffee table, bigger than ... life. I turned on the television, switched to various channels to see if there was anything worth watching, then turned it off. I resisted the temptation to look at my watch.

I sat back down on the couch and picked up the book of short stories and read until my eyelids got heavy. I stood up and picked up the suitcase and the Python and brought them into the bedroom with me. I set the suitcase on the floor next to the bed, put my weapon on the end table, checked the bedroom phone to make sure it was plugged in and had a dial tone, undressed, climbed into bed, and went to sleep a few seconds after I closed my eyes.

SIXTEEN

THE suitcase was still sitting there by the bed when I woke up the next morning at eight o'clock. I threw on a robe and went outside, picked up the newspaper, checked the weather—it looked like it was going to rain—and scoped out the street for anything out of the usual, different cars, strange people, but saw nothing. There was no sign of Farns either. I knew he was out there someplace, but there was no evidence of him, nor his car—a pea-green '74 Pontiac with a huge front end and massive fenders that you could spot from a mile way. Back inside, I took a quick shower, got dressed, and fixed breakfast. Cereal and toast. I checked the time. It was 8:45. It looked like it was going to be a long day.

I drank three cups of hot black coffee with my cereal, and I read the paper. I read the paper twice, front to back. It wasn't that interesting. It was something to do. The national news was the same old shit and basically so was the sports. I checked to see how my baseball team was doing. They were in last place in their division. I read the local news with more interest, and scrutinized the obituaries slowly and carefully, checking out the people's names and their ages.

It was the one section of the paper that I read with great care. Without really knowing why, it was something I had done ever since Catherine's death.

In the entertainment section I saw that the 7:30 movie

at the Vogue on Lexington Road was an old Orson Welles flick, *Touch of Evil*. It figured. Written and directed by Welles, photographed by Russell Metty, starring Welles and Charlton Heston, Janet Leigh, and Marlene Dietrich, with Joseph Cotten and Akim Tamiroff, it was a wild crime thriller full of weird scenes and offbeat dialog, and incredible camera shots. I had seen it once years ago and had been waiting for it to return to a revival house ever since.

Disgusted, I turned to the classifieds and starting reading the Help Wanted ads. There were ads for accountants and cashiers and delivery people, for engineers and legal secretaries and R.N.s and purchasing agents, but none for private eyes. And all the ads said "Send Resume and Cover letter." I tried to picture what a private eye's resume would sound like.

Professional sleuth. Primary responsibility to investigate cases no one in their right mind would take. Proven ability to follow up leads, shadow suspects, discover the obvious clues. Solid background in ransom exchanges, stakeouts, and sleazy situations. Work well under pressure and against impossible deadlines. Able to interface with all levels of clientele, from the very rich to the very crazy. Extensive experience sitting around waiting for calls that never come. Proficient in use of small arms. Qualified on Colt Python. Certified fistfighter.

The regular ads sounded good. They offered excellent pay and benefits, retirement plans and health insurance, all the goodies that came with working at a normal occupation for a large corporation. Maybe the thing to do was go back to school and do a mid-life career change. Get a degree in business administration and be somebody's accountant or production manager. I considered it. For about two seconds.

I folded up the paper, went into the front room, and switched on the television. I spent the rest of the day watching game shows and soap operas and talk shows and children's programs. Whoever said television was a wasteland was being kind. In the middle of the day I called and had a pizza delivered. I ate it in the front room while I sat in a kind of trance and watched Donahue or Geraldo or somebody. At five in the afternoon the phone rang and I got up and switched off the set, and picked up the phone.

It was McGraw.

"If you want me to, I'll hang right up."

"Don't do that," I said. "I'm kinda glad to hear your voice."

"You're glad to hear my voice?" she repeated. "Are you joking?"

"What's happening out in the world there?"

"You talk as if you're on a desert island, or something."

"I feel like I'm on an island. I'm going stir crazy."

"No calls?"

"No calls."

"Where's Farnsworth?"

"He's out there somewhere. He's supposed to be watching my back."

"It's starting to rain," McGraw said.

I looked out the window. She was right. It was beginning to sprinkle lightly.

"I better get off the line," McGraw said.

"Yeah."

"Hey, Rhineheart?"

"Huh?"

"Be careful."

"Yeah."

The line went dead.

I stretched out on the couch and took a nap. When I woke it was past seven and the room had grown dark. I got up and went over to the window. It was raining steadily now and night was falling. I went into the kitchen, put on a pot of Irish tea, and rummaged around in one of the drawers until I found a deck of cards. I sat at the kitchen table, sipping tea and playing solitaire. I played for hours, hand after hand. When the phone finally rang I looked at my watch and was surprised to see that it was 11:50, ten minutes to midnight. I walked into the front room and picked up the phone.

"Pay attention now." It was the same voice. "I'm not going to repeat this. It's 11:51 now. As soon we finish talking, you get in your car and drive over to the shopping strip at the corner of Berry Boulevard and Seventh Street Road. Don't take the expressway. Take Eastern Parkway. There's an outdoor phone stand on the far side of the all-night donut shop. We'll call you there in exactly twenty minutes. Don't be late" was the last thing the voice said before the connection was broken.

I hung up the phone, strapped on my shoulder holster, took out my Python, and broke open the chamber. I had a full load, two regulars, two hollow points, and two bullets that would pierce the armor on a small tank. My motto was Be prepared. I got a windbreaker out of the closet, slipped it on, and zipped it up. I went into the bedroom and picked up the suitcase—it still felt heavy—and brought it back to the front room. I opened the front door, stepped outside, set the suitcase down, closed and locked the apartment door, picked up the suitcase, and carried it down the sidewalk to the Maverick. I went around to the trunk, set the suitcase down on the wet pavement, unlocked the trunk, picked up the suitcase, laid it in the trunk next to the jack and the spare, and closed and locked the trunk.

I slid in under the wheel and started the car. The engine sounded funny. I don't know anything about cars, but I knew the engine didn't sound right. I'd have to get someone to look at it. I pulled away from the curb and at the end of the block turned right at Bonnycastle.

I took Bonnycastle to Bardstown Road and turned

right again. There was hardly any traffic. The streets were slick and black, glistening. The wipers made a slurping sound across the windshield. The back and side windows had fogged up some and, except for an occasional headlight, I couldn't see anything behind me. If Farnsworth was backing me up, he was doing it invisibly.

I motored down Bardstown Road, passing the closed fronts of antique shops and upscale restaurants. I passed the Uptown Movie Theater and turned left at Eastern Parkway. I was pointed west now, following the route the voice on the phone had given me. The thieves, I guessed, were probably watching at certain points along the way. To ensure that no one was following me. I drove carefully, thirty-five miles an hour, and kept to the right lane. It was no time to be stopped by the police for anything.

At the intersection of Eastern Parkway and Third Street, I turned left under the viaduct, then took a right at Winkler Avenue. I eased the Maverick over into the left-hand lane and came to a stop for a red light at the corner of Fourth Street. The rain beat steadily down. Left, right, straight ahead, and behind, the streets were deserted, without traffic or pedestrians. The light changed to green and I tapped the accelerator. The Maverick lurched forward. I switched lanes again as Winkler curved into Taylor Boulevard, turned right at the corner of Berry, and sped down Berry to Seventh Street Road.

The shopping center was just past the intersection of Seventh and Berry. A line of a dozen dark storefronts, a large well-lighted parking area, and at one end, set off by itself, a small all-night donut shop whose windows gleamed with light. There were half a dozen cars parked near the donut shop. I pulled the Maverick around the far side and saw the outdoor phone—located in a stand that adjoined the building. I nudged the Maverick into an empty parking space nearby.

THE QUEEN'S MARE 97

I rolled the window partway down. It was still raining heavily. There didn't seem to be any need to secure the phone. Who would want to use an outdoor phone in this kind of weather? But sure enough, in a few minutes, a tall guy in a baseball cap came out of the donut shop and headed straight for the phone.

I didn't see him immediately, and by the time I did and got out of the car and over to the phone, he had dropped his money in the slot, had the receiver in his hand, and was dialing a number.

He watched me approach with an irritable look on his face.

"I'd like to talk to you for a minute," I said.

"What about?" His tone was unfriendly.

"I'm expecting an important call," I said. "I want to use the phone. Would you mind hanging up?"

He gave me a look of scornful amusement. "You need to use the phone, huh? Well, that's tough shit, fuckface." He turned his back on me.

Fuckface? I considered the situation. My watch said 12:11. Twenty-one minutes since the thief had called. I had no idea how he would react if the line was busy, but I couldn't take any chances.

The way I saw it, I didn't have too many choices. I could get physical and separate the man from the phone, but a tussle, even if it was a slight one and over with quickly, would consume too much time. I unzipped the windbreaker and took the Python out of the holster. The guy was speaking into the receiver now. He was saying, "Listen to me, Mona, you shithead bitch, you. Pay fucking attention—"

I tapped him on the shoulder and when he swung around I stuck the Python in his face.

"Tell Mona goodnight and hang up the phone."

The color drained out of the guy's face. He opened his mouth to speak, but no words came out. I reached over, took the phone out of his hand, and spoke into it. "Mona," I said, "this asshole you're talking to will call you back later. And Mona, he apologizes for calling you bad names." I hung the receiver on the hook.

"Take off," I told the guy. He turned quickly and sprinted across the parking lot to a car, jumped in, and peeled away. I didn't feel all that great about what I'd just done. I took no pleasure in scaring people, even if they were assholes, but sometimes things like that had to be done. As I was putting away my weapon, the phone rang. I grabbed the receiver and put it to my ear.

"You done fine so far, friend. Keep doing what you're told and this whole thing will soon be over. Turn around now and head back the way you came. When you get back to where Eastern Parkway runs into the expressway, get on 65 and head south. Just past the Bullitt County line, you'll see an exit for State Highway 6. The exit number is 27. Take it and head east for two miles and you'll come up on an old abandoned riding stables on your left. There's a gravel driveway entrance. There's two buildings, the office and the stables. Pull right in there and park in front of the *first* building, the office. You got that?"

"The first building," I said.

"That's right," the voice said. "You pull in there and turn off your motor and your lights. You'll see a yellow horse van parked near the stable building. You sit there and wait exactly five minutes, then get out of the car and open your trunk and unlock the suitcase."

"Wait a minute," I said.

"Shut the fuck up, and do exactly what I'm telling you," the voice said. "Or the old lady'll never see the mare and the foal alive again. You understand what I'm telling you?"

"I understand," I said.

"Unlock the suitcase like I said. Leave the trunk open. Then get back in your car. Wait five more minutes, then get out of your car and go over to the van, which is where the mare and the foal will be. Now hang

THE QUEEN'S MARE

up and go directly out to the stables. Make no stops. You're being watched." The line went dead.

I stood there a moment with the dead phone in my hand, feeling the rain on my face. I had made some bad moves before, taken some wrong cases, but this one was sheer folly. There was almost no way it could turn out right. I hung up the phone and walked back to the car.

The rain continued steadily as I retraced my route—along Berry to Taylor, up Taylor to Winkler, Third Street, Eastern Parkway. I swung up on the expressway, heading south.

I hunched forward over the wheel, concentrating on the road. I switched on the radio, tuned it to a late-night station that featured a female disc jockey with a silky voice who played old-timey jazz records into the middle of the night.

Traffic was light on I–65, but I stayed in the slow lane and kept a cool foot on the gas. Every now and then a huge semi would come roaring past on my left. I had been on the expressway for twenty minutes when, just south of the Bullitt County line, exit 27 loomed up on my right. I wheeled the Maverick down the exit, a series of tight curves that twisted back under the expressway and deposited me on State Highway 6, a two-lane asphalt road that ran east and west.

I pointed the Maverick east. On both sides of the road the landscape was a combination of open fields and farmland broken up by rural business establishments—liquor stores, gas stations, small grocery stores. After a few miles I saw, on my left, a faded sign that read: B LL T Co TY R D NG St B ES. A gravel driveway formed a semicircle across the front of several small buildings. Although it was dark and hard to see, I could make out a light-colored horse van parked in front of the second building. I could also see what looked like a riding ring encircled by a plank fence.

I turned into the gravel driveway and pulled to a stop

in front of the first building, a small wooden garage-sized structure. The second building, twenty yards farther along the driveway, was a stable with a shingled roof and a dozen horse stalls. Both buildings were weatherbeaten and unpainted. The van, which was yellow, wasn't hitched to anything.

I shut off my lights and the motor. It was pitch black now, dark the way it gets when you're in the country, and, except for the steady patter of the rain, quiet.

I waited exactly five minutes, then opened the door, and got out of the car. I walked over and peered into the open back of the van.

It was empty, which meant that the whole thing was a double cross, a set up of some kind. The thieves must have—I heard a shuffling sound behind me. I started to turn when something hard slammed into the back of my head. It was as if a dark wave of water was rolling over me. I felt myself going under and falling slowly . . . slowly . . . beneath the surface of consciousness.

When I came to, I was lying on my back on the wet ground. A bright light was shining into my eyes. The light went out suddenly and I found myself staring up at the sharp angles of a familiar face, a familiar pair of bloodshot eyes.

"Kid?" the face said. "You okay?"

Farnsworth. The old pro.

"I got hit on the head," I said. "From behind."

Farnsworth nodded. "You got suckered." His face crinkled into what was probably a smile. Then he sobered up and peered solemnly down at me. "Your pupils look okay though," he said. "I don't think there's a concussion."

"It hurts like a sonofabitch," I said.

"Well sure," Farnsworth said, "I bet it does." He was carrying a flashlight and he gestured with it. "But what are you gonna do? Lie there and moan about it all night?"

"I might, yeah," I said. I held up my hand and Farnsworth helped me to my feet. Momentarily dizzy, I had to reach out and grab Farnsworth's arm to steady myself.

I shook my head clear and took a look around me. The horse van was in the same place. I could see now that one of the back tires was missing and the hitch was all but buried in the ground. The van was a permanent fixture of the place. The thieves had never intended to make an exchange.

I looked over at the Maverick. The trunk had been forced open. Farnsworth clicked on the flashlight and directed its beam on the trunk. The suitcase was gone.

I spoke the words out loud: "They got the money."

Farnsworth nodded and clicked off the light. "I got here two minutes behind you and about one minute late. I saw a red Toyota pickup go past me on the highway. Late model. This year's or last year's. Looked like two people in it. Couldn't make out if they was men or women. I don't even know if they came out of here, but it was the only vehicle on the highway. I couldn't see the license plate well enough to get even a partial."

"I lost the money," I said.

Farnsworth nodded. "Sure you did, but that's no reason to get down on yourself."

"It's *not*?"

Farnsworth shook his head. "It was an impossible situation. They controlled everything. All you could do was give it your best shot." He beckoned. "C'mere, kid."

I followed the old man across the gravel to the other side of the stable. There was a small cleared area, large enough to park a car or a truck. Farnsworth clicked on the flashlight and pointed at the ground. "Here's where they parked," he said, indicating a set of tire tracks.

Farnsworth squatted suddenly and picked something off the ground. He straightened up and then stooped down and picked up something else. He held out his palm and angled the flashlight so I could see what was in his hand.

In the center of the old man's wrinkled palm lay two soggy cigarette butts and the torn, wet cover of a matchbook.

"What you got there, Farns?"

"Clues, buddy boy. Gen-you-wine arthentic clues. The cigs are Camel Filters, which I believe you told me is the kind Eddie Walker smokes, and the matchbook is from a club called Greenstreets. Does that ring a bell?"

"Greenstreets is Graves's place," I said. "Shirley Beaumont is part owner."

Farnsworth nodded again. "Things are getting curiouser." He looked at the items on his hand again. "You think these are plants, kid?"

I shrugged and felt the sore place on my head. I needed to see about that. I looked up at the night sky and realized for the first time since I'd come to that it had stopped raining. "You know what, Farns?"

"Yeah," Farns said, "I know."

"I fucked up," I said.

Farnsworth nodded one more time. "Bigger than shit," he said. "What I'd call a royal fuck-up."

SEVENTEEN

"They got *all* the money?"

"Shut up, McGraw."

"The whole million dollars?"

"You're getting on my nerves."

McGraw said, "Hold still," and swabbed at a cut near my right ear. I was sitting in my office swivel chair. McGraw hovered over me, an iodine bottle in one hand, a Q-tip in the other. Farnsworth had gone home to catch some sleep.

"That smarts," I said, wincing.

"Of course it smarts," McGraw said. "The back of your head looks like its been in a blender," she added. "What did they hit you with?"

"I don't know," I said, "but it was hard."

"What you need to do," McGraw said, "is have a doctor look at it."

I shook my head. "Can't do that. I have to go out to Ashtree and tell Mrs. Beaumont what happened."

McGraw rolled her eyes ceilingward. "I don't envy you that job."

I shrugged and started to say something, but McGraw threw up a hand. "I know." She growled out a weak imitation of my voice: "Man's got to do what he's got to do."

"Go home and get some sleep," I said.

After McGraw left, I sat in the office and waited until daybreak to call Ashtree and tell them I was coming.

When I got there, Hattie Beaumont, Diane Carter, and Wallace Thornton were waiting for me in the library.

I told them how the thing had come down. Without any frills. When I was finished there was a long silence, which was broken finally by Wallace Thornton. "Why did you not carry out the kidnappers' instructions? Why didn't you open the trunk as you were told?"

I said, "I thought it would be best to check out the van first."

"They gave you explicit instructions, did they not?"

"Yeah," I admitted, "they sure did."

"Instead of cooperating with them," Thornton said, "you acted independently—recklessly, I might add."

I didn't say anything.

"You gave us your assurances," Thornton said.

I had made no assurances, but I said nothing.

Hattie Beaumont spoke. Her voice was stiff and weighted with disappointment. "I did not think, Mr. Rhineheart, that you would fail us in this matter."

I made no reply. What was there to say? The old woman might have crumpled to the floor in a faint, and I couldn't have felt any worse.

Diane Carter looked distressed.

Leaning heavily on her cane, Hattie Beaumont walked over to the big armchair and eased herself into it. In the corner of my eye I caught a movement in the rear of the room. I looked up and noticed for the first time that Paige was there, standing near the French doors, and that Miss Hackett was sitting in a rocking chair in the corner, bent over her needles.

I spoke to Hattie Beaumont: "I screwed things up pretty badly," I said. "But it wasn't all my fault. The way it was laid out, it was a no-win situation to begin with."

Hattie Beaumont looked pained. She cast a look at Wallace Thornton, who said, "By God, sir, haven't you done enough? Your performance tonight was not satisfactory. Must you add to it by attempting to excuse it?"

I kept my eyes on Hattie Beaumont. "I want you to know that I'll find the mare and the foal for you, Mrs. Beaumont. And I'll get the money back, too."

Hattie Beaumont wouldn't look at me.

"Mr. Rhineheart," Thornton said, "Ashtree Farms no longer requires your services. Your relationship with us is terminated, as of now."

Diane Carter looked as if she was about to speak, but she remained silent.

I nodded, then turned and left the room.

Outside, my car was parked next to the farm van. I slid behind the wheel of the Maverick, started it up, and headed down the farm road toward the main gate.

I drove past a cluster of barns and came up on the guard station, which was being manned now by the same pair of guards I had encountered on Monday.

I wheeled the Maverick through the main entrance onto the highway, and hesitated. A left would take me to Eddie Walker's apartment, but the chances of finding him there were slim to none. I turned right, heading back downtown to the office. Walker's place could wait for the moment. I needed to talk to Farnsworth and McGraw, get my bearings.

As I drove, I thought about the promise I'd made to Hattie Beaumont. It was big talk for a "lowlife, half-ass gunshoe" as Katz had called me. Especially one who had no resources to speak of: a small office in an old building, a secretary who couldn't type or file, and an old pro who was past his prime. With the exception of Walker, I didn't have a single genuine suspect. A glimpse of a red pickup truck, a couple of soggy cigarette butts, and a matchbook were my only clues. On top of this, the Queen of England was due to arrive in three days. To keep my promise to Hattie Beaumont, I was going to need a big streak of luck, or a miracle. The trouble with that was that I'd run out of luck a long time ago—right around the time I'd stopped believing in miracles.

Downtown, I found a parking spot in front of the office and climbed the stairs to the second floor. McGraw sat behind her desk. Farnsworth was asleep in my chair with his feet up and his hat, a beat-up old-timey fedora, over his eyes. His snore sounded like the steady buzz of a lawnmower engine. I took a client's chair. McGraw handed me a cup of coffee and a chocolate Bismark.

"Any calls?"

"Two: Sergeant Katz and Shirley Beaumont. Katz wants you to call him back. Shirley Beaumont wants you to come by her house sometime today, if possible."

"Any mail?"

"Bills and junk."

"Shitcan it."

"I already did."

"We got fired," I said.

McGraw nodded. "I figured as much. So what are we going to do first? Look for the horses, or go after the thieves?"

"We find the thieves," I said, "and we'll find the mare and the foal *and* the money."

"I know why you're doing this," McGraw said.

"I'm doing it," I said, "because you can't let someone burn you and rip you off the way I got burned and ripped off. Word gets around on that and no one will hire you for anything."

"That's not the real reason you're doing it," McGraw said. "The *real* reason is because getting the money back and finding the horses and the thieves is what a private sleuth is supposed to do. It's like a code, or something."

Sleuth? Code? What the hell was McGraw talking about? She'd been reading too many books lately. "I got a job for you," I said.

"More research stuff," McGraw said with disgust.

I shook my head. "This is the real thing."

McGraw's face brightened. "Oh boy!"

"I want you to do a little stakeout number on Wallace Thornton. His address is in the phone book. His office is on the eleventh floor of Professional Towers."

McGraw made a face. "Stakeouts are almost as bad as research. They're so boring. I don't even know what Thornton looks like. Which means I'll have to do some more research to get a photograph so I can go stake him out, which isn't that much better than research in the first place anyway."

"Life is tough," I said. I wrote the name *John Dixon* on a slip of paper and handed it to McGraw. "On your way to get the photograph I need you to stop off and see this guy."

McGraw tapped the paper. "Who's John Dixon?"

"He's in the equine insurance business. He writes the insurance policies on Ashtree Farms. I want you to find out what kind of policy he wrote on Winterset."

"He a suspect?"

I shrugged. "I don't know."

"What about Hattie Beaumont? She a suspect?"

"Sure."

"How come?"

"'Cause we need all the suspects we can get."

"Ain't that the truth," Farnsworth said from under his hat. He dropped his feet to the floor, pushed the fedora back off his face, and leaned back in the chair. He squinted around the room, smacked his lips loudly, and said, "I could use a cup of java about right now."

McGraw pointed to a white paper sack on her desk. "No one has used the word *java* since 1949," she said.

Farnsworth pushed himself out of the chair, walked over and lifted a cup out of the bag. He returned to the swivel chair, where after snapping off the lid and taking a big slurp, he wrestled a pack of cigarettes out of an inner pocket, lit one up, and inhaled a big cloud of smoke. When he spoke it was as if he was talking to himself. "That was one hell of a year, 1949," he said. "I was in my twenties, had two or three girliefriends, all of them built like brick shithouses. I drove a new Ford and had an apartment over by the racetrack. That was the year I had a horse payed one hundred and twelve dollars and forty cents. For two, that is. It was also the year I solved the Fontaine Ferry Murders. Fontaine Ferry, for those of you who don't know their local history, was the name of an amusement park in the West End. The case was a real doozy," he said to McGraw, who was staring at him openmouthed. "Sometime when we got some time I'll tell you about it." He turned to me. "You want me to keep an eye on Graves, or what?"

"We don't have a client on this one anymore, old man."

"You ain't telling me nothing I don't already know, kid."

"I can cover your beer and gas money, but that's about it."

Farnsworth shrugged. "I worked for expenses before. We got to finish this thing up, don't we? When's the Queen gonna be here?"

"Sunday," McGraw said. The *Courier Journal* was lying on her desk. She picked it up and read, "'English royalty will ascend on the state once again when Queen Elizabeth II of England will visit the state for the second time in the last four years. The British monarch will be in Louisville on Sunday, May 18, for a two-day stay, during which time she will be the guest of Hattie Beaumont, the prominent Kentucky horseowner, at Ashtree Farms in Prospect.

"'Buckingham Palace said the visit will be private, with no public appearances planned. The palace said there was no word on who would accompany the Queen. Hattie Beaumont, the grand dame of Kentucky Thoroughbred racing, could not be reached for comment yesterday on the Queen's expected visit.'"

THE QUEEN'S MARE

"One of the things I been thinking about all night," Farnsworth said, "is why they didn't return the horses. It don't make sense. It would have been in their best interests to return the mare and foal, but from the way it happened it doesn't look as if they ever intended to give them back. Pretty soon, when this thing becomes public they're going to be holding on to some pretty hot property. Going to be hard to hide."

"Unless they've already done something," I said.

"Such as?"

"Disposed of the mare and the foal."

"Yeah, but they wouldn't be that dumb, would they?"

I shrugged. "Who knows? Maybe they're crazy."

"You think there might be some other factor operating?" Farns said.

"Such as?"

Farns shrugged. "Maybe it might be something more than or something *besides* a kidnapping. Kidnapping may just be part of it. Maybe someone's out to get Ashtree Farms."

"Or the Beaumonts," I said.

"Or both."

"What does that mean?" McGraw said. "Is there a chance that somebody is going to get—I don't know—hurt or even killed, or something?"

"Let's hope not," I said.

I looked over at Farnsworth, who had buried his nose in the coffee. He believed that it was bad luck to talk about killing.

"Old man," I said, "you think you can keep an eye on Curtis Graves without being spotted?"

"I can give it a try," he said. The truth was he was the master when it came to shadowing people. Almost impossible to spot, he had a knack for fading into whatever background was around. In the old days he was called "The Magician" because of his ability to disappear at will.

Farns slurped some coffee, inhaled more smoke, stood up, put his cigarette out in the coffee, dropped the cup in the wastebasket, and began to move slowly toward the door.

I told him to keep in touch.

"See you later, kid... girlie." He disappeared out into the hall.

"Can I call you 'girlie,' too?" I asked McGraw.

She showed me her fist. "Just try it one time." She handed me a slip of paper with a phone number on it. "Katz's office."

"A lot of secretaries," I said, "would dial the number, get the other person on the line, *then* give the phone to their boss."

"You got a broken hand, or something?"

I dialed Katz's number.

"Katz, Homicide."

"This is Rhineheart. You call me about something?"

"Peeper, your telephone etiquette"—Katz pronounced it et-tea-kett—"is atrocious. You're supposed to introduce yourself. You ain't supposed to jump on somebody when they pick up the receiver."

"What do you want, Katz?"

"Just a friendly call, Peeper. Heard you got knocked on the head, lost some serious money, and didn't get the horses back. That right?"

"This what you call *friendly*, Katz?"

"The figure I heard was one million in cold cash."

"Sounds like an awful lot of money," I said.

"Way too much to trust to a gumshoe," Katz said. "Especially a half-ass one."

"You pissed off at me for calling you a name, Peeper? Don't be. Don't take that stuff personal. We're old buddies, and I thought maybe as an old friend, and now that you're off the case officially, you might want to be a little more cooperative."

"I always try to cooperate with the authorities, Sergeant."

THE QUEEN'S MARE

"Sure you do," Katz said with heavy sarcasm. "How about confirming a few facts, Peep?"

"Be glad to."

"Word is you got fired, but it didn't stick. Understand you're gonna stay on the case? That correct?"

"No comment."

"*No comment?* That's what they say to reporters, Peep, not cops."

"I gotta go, Katz. I'm a busy man."

"Keep me informed on this, Rhineheart. Don't be running around half-cocked on your own. And don't do anything to piss me off, Peeper."

"Goodbye, Katz." I hung up.

McGraw handed me a slip of paper.

"What's this?"

"The address of Thoroughbred Employment."

The employment agency that got Walker the job at Ashtree. It was a place to start.

EIGHTEEN

THOROUGHBRED Employment Agency was on the second floor of a vine-covered white stucco building on LaGrange Road. The office manager's name was Brown. A tall, reedlike man with thin lips and thick glasses. "As a client of ours, Mr. Walker is protected by our policy of strict confidentiality. We are not able to provide any information concerning his employment, and we certainly cannot let you see his personnel file, Detective"—Brown squinted at the card I'd given to him—"Katz."

I sighed and shook my head. "The Chief will be awfully disappointed," I said. "He was hoping we could clear this up quickly on an informal basis. I'm afraid he's going to lose his temper over this. In the event your response to our request was unsatisfactory, the Chief asked me to find out the name of your immediate superior."

"*My* immediate superior?"

"Correct."

"I . . ." Brown gulped. "I report directly to the operations manager, Mr. Kaufman."

I pointed to a blank memo pad on Brown's desk. "Can I borrow a sheet of that and a pen?"

Brown handed me a pen. I tore a sheet off the pad and wrote *Kaufman, Op Mgr* on it.

I handed Brown his pen and got to my feet. "Well,

THE QUEEN'S MARE

I'm sorry you couldn't have been more helpful, Mr. Brown."

Brown stood up quickly. "Just a second, Sergeant Katz. Maybe there is a way we can do this more informally. I see no real harm in that."

I sat back down. "The Chief will be pleased, Mr. Brown."

I sat in the Maverick in the parking lot outside Thoroughbred Employment Agency studying Eddie Walker's employment file.

Thoroughbred Employment Agency
Employment Record

NAME: Edward J. Walker   SSN: 471–46–8879
DOB: 3/12/57
CURRENT ADDRESS: 2134 Fairview
Rent/own: Rent
How long lived there: 6 mo
NAME OF NEAREST RELATIVE (Relationship): Betty Walker (wife-ex)
ADDRESS: Valley Station Mobile Home Park 14235 River End Rd.
DRIVERS LICENSE: Yes: x   No:
MAKE OF CAR: '78 Mercury
LICENSE NO: KY 43-289 (Jefferson County)

RECORD OF PREVIOUS EMPLOYMENT:
COMPANY: Brookview Farms
LOCATION: Lexington, KY
FROM/TO: 7/87–2/89
JOB TITLE: Stablehand/Assistant Groom
REASONS FOR LEAVING: Resigned for better position

COMPANY: Jack Kruger Racing Stable
LOCATION: Louisville, KY
FROM/TO: 6/85–7/86

JOB TITLE: Hotwalker/Stablehelp
REASONS FOR LEAVING: Disagreement with supervisor

EDUCATION: 10th grade
TECHNICAL SKILLS (if any): None
MILITARY SERVICE: U.S. Navy 1972–1974
CRIMINAL RECORD (List all arrests for felonies): None
REFERENCES:

James Bergman, Atty.   Joe Brown, Mgr.
Roth and Williams   Kruger Stable
Louisville, KY   Louisville, KY
          Ted Fowler, Foreman
          Brookview Farms
          Lexington, KY

With the Queen due on Sunday, I didn't have the time to check out Walker's references or trace him through old jobs. The thing on the paper that looked like it might be the most useful was his ex-wife's address.

I started up the Maverick and drove over to Walker's apartment. The landlord hadn't seen Walker for a week. A small gray-haired man in a dirty T-shirt, the landlord had a week's silver stubble on his cheeks, and a pensive solemn air about him, as if he had important things on his mind. "The bastard left owing me last month's," he said, scratching his stubble.

For a twenty-dollar bill, he let me look around Walker's apartment. I took my time—sometimes you had to force yourself to be deliberate when the area you were searching was small—and searched the place thoroughly and methodically, but the only thing I found that seemed significant was a wrinkled piece of notepaper with the message *I'd like to talk to you some more about that matter we discussed. Don't worry, I'll make it worth your while*. The message was signed with the initials *LT*. It didn't take a detective to figure out that

THE QUEEN'S MARE 115

the initials referred to America's most famous horse trainer.

I found the note in the bottom of a garbage bag in Walker's kitchen. As I was digging through the bag, I thought about Thornton's term *highest levels* for the status of his bank connections. Levels. The word meant a lot of different things. Some cases had levels below levels and you had to dig deep to turn up the secrets. There was that kind of level, and there was the level you operated on, which is what Thornton had been talking about. In those terms the bottom of the garbage bag was the level where most private eyes did their work.

The landlord was no help when it came to providing information about Walker's habits or friends. He said he encountered Walker only infrequently, didn't know who visited him or anything else about him.

Logically, my next stop was the address of Walker's ex-wife, but Dixie Highway was on the other side of town, a thirty-minute drive, and Shirley Beaumont's place was on the way. I decided to stop there first.

Hattie's oldest granddaughter lived in a fashionable neighborhood that bordered a small park in the central part of the city. A wide strip of grass divided the street, which was lined on both sides by large overhanging trees. In the middle of the block an ornate bronze fountain spouted water. The houses were huge, elaborate Victorian and Italianate mansions replete with turrets, cupolas, spires, and gargoyles.

Shirley Beaumont's place was three stories of gray stone topped off with a cupola. There were columns and stained-glass windows and a veranda that swept around the side of the house. Marble steps led up to a front door that looked like it belonged on a bank.

I hit the bell and after a short wait the door was answered by a young muscular woman in sweats who introduced herself as "Terri, Shirley's trainer," and took my hand in a bone-crushing grip as if we were in a strongperson's handshaking contest.

I was tempted to say, "Ease up, motherfucker," but I bit the words back, and let her do a squeeze job on my fingers. She had a good grip and she seemed to be getting a big kick out of it.

"I'm here to see Ms. Beaumont," I said. When she let go of my hand, pride or something—what McGraw would probably call my male chauvinist piggishness—kept me from flexing the numbness out of my fingers.

"Terri," who had tight brown curls, nodded and said, "Shirley's in the gym." She led me down a hallway past rooms filled with antiques and overstuffed furniture into a sun porch that had been converted into a "gym." It contained a hot tub, sets of weights, a stationary bike, a rowing machine, and Nautilus equipment. The floor was padded. Shirley Beaumont was in shorts that showed a lot of thigh and a T-shirt. Charlotte had accused her of not having "tits" but Charlotte was wrong. Shirley's breasts were where they were supposed to be, small but firm, and shaped like melons. Her body was trim and hard, glistening with sweat. I was struck again by the recognition that all the Beaumont women were good-looking. Shirley was in the middle of a set of bench presses, taking deep breaths, and extending the weight up above her.

"She's up to one seventy-five," Terri whispered proudly. I nodded as if I knew what she was talking about and was impressed. Big fucking deal. I couldn't resist saying, "Is her handshake as good as yours?"

Terri glared at me in response.

Shirley Beaumont eased the weight back into its slot and sat up. She smiled politely at me, then warmly at Terri, who threw her a towel, said, "I'll be in the pool," and left the room without a word to me. I was beginning to feel like the odd man out.

"I got a message that you wanted to see me," I told Shirley Beaumont.

She nodded. "Yes."

"What for?"

She shook her head in mock admiration. "You don't play around. You go right to the meat of it, don't you?"

I shrugged. "Why play around?"

"Why indeed? You have a point, Mr. Rhineheart. I want to hire you. I need a bodyguard. I've recently received some... death threats. They're similar to the threats that Grandmother and Charlotte received. Essentially the same message. Unlike them, however, I take the threats quite seriously. I believe that someone is out to do members of the family harm."

It was, of course, the first that I had heard about any death threats. I was careful not to appear surprised. "You said they had the same message as the other threats. What did they say exactly?"

"It was a man's voice, and it seemed to be amplified by something. It was as if he were speaking into a megaphone. He said almost the same thing that he had said to Grandmother and Charlotte. He said, 'It is time for Justice on the Beaumonts, or *against* the Beaumonts. Your turn to die is coming. Soon.' He repeated the word soon and drew it out. It was frightening, Mr. Rhineheart. That's why I called you. I want to hire your services as a bodyguard. I want someone there to protect me if these threats materialize."

"I'll give you a number to call," I said. "Johnny Reardon at Midtown Investigations does personal security jobs. He's good at it."

"I don't want other people, Mr. Rhineheart. I want *you*."

"Why? I screwed up the job I was doing for your grandmother."

"I don't think you screwed it up. I think you were given an impossible assignment. The truth is, I like your style. You're straight and direct and to the point. If you say you're going to do a thing, you do it. I think you could protect me if any real danger surfaced."

"Yeah, well, I don't do bodyguard work," I said, "and besides, I'm committed to something else."

"You're not talking about still finding the mare and the foal, are you?"

"Yeah."

"Correct me if I'm wrong," Shirley Beaumont said, "but didn't Grandmother terminate you this morning? Aren't you officially off the case, as they say?"

"Technically, maybe, but in every way that matters I'll be on the case until it's over."

"That's really admirable, Mr. Rhineheart, but I'll double your usual fee if you work for me."

"It's tempting," I said, and it *was*. Mildly. I could forget about the fucking mare and foal and stop worrying about the Queen's arrival. I could drop chasing around after some assistant groom and lie back and make some easy bucks. But then there was the promise I had made to Hattie Beaumont. And there was what had happened to me last night. I had to take care of that. "Sorry," I said.

"But it's absurd to remain on the case," Shirley Beaumont said. "You don't even have a client."

I shrugged. "Sometimes it works out that way."

"Will you at least give my request some consideration?" she asked.

"I'll think about it," I said. "In the meantime, here's Reardon's number." I took out a pen and wrote the number on the back of one of my cards and held it out to her. She pointed to a small table. "Set it there, would you please?" I put the card on the table.

Shirley Beaumont stood up. "I won't keep you any longer, Mr. Rhineheart. I know you're busy. Please reconsider my request. I'd feel a good deal safer with you aboard. I'll show you to the front door."

As we walked back down the hallway, I said, "I got a visit from Curtis Graves the other day."

I had been hoping to catch her by surprise but Shirley Beaumont didn't blink. "Who?"

"You don't know Curtis?"

"The name doesn't sound familiar."

"That's funny," I said. "I thought you two were partners in a West End nightclub."

Shirley smiled and waved a hand. "Oh, *that* Curtis. Of course. Curtis and I are old and dear friends. Among other things, Curtis is my connection to the, uh, minority business community."

"Curtis seems to know about all the goings-on out at Ashtree. He offered me some help."

"In light of what happened, maybe you should have taken it."

"Maybe."

"When you turned him down, I hope you didn't hurt his feelings. Curtis is very sensitive. Thin-skinned, you might say."

"Curtis also asked after you."

"The dear boy. How nice of him." We had reached the front door. She opened it and we stepped out onto the porch.

"Curtis gave me the impression that you two were partners in more than just a nightclub. Curtis acted as if your interests and his were more or less identical."

Shirley Beaumont smiled a knowing smile. "Do you know Curtis very well, Mr. Rhineheart?"

"Slightly," I said.

"You are aware of what he does for a living?"

"I know he's a pimp and a drug dealer and I know that he'll shylock some money out now and then."

Shirley Beaumont made a face. "What a horrible term. I believe it has anti-Semitic connotations. However, it's true. Curtis loans money to people in need. At exorbitant rates. There, in a nutshell, you have our relationship. Curtis is my Shylock. To put it simply, I owe him a good deal of money. So, in a way, you're right. His interests ought to be my interests. If anything happened to me..."

"Curtis might be the answer to your protection problem," I suggested. "Maybe you could call him."

"Interesting idea," Shirley Beaumont said. "On the other hand, and here's where it begins to get complicated, Mr. Rhineheart, I'm not absolutely sure that Curtis isn't involved with whoever's making the threats."

I had no response to that. It was one more item to add to the heap of information that was piling up in my head. I said goodbye and headed down the marble steps to my car.

NINETEEN

Valley Station Mobile Home Park was located on a sideroad off Dixie Highway. Betty Walker's trailer was a squat gray aluminum model that sat on cinder blocks. A yellow Chevette was parked alongside it.

I knocked on the door and after a minute it was yanked open by a slim sandy-haired woman in jeans and a halter top. She was the woman in the framed photograph on Walker's dresser, and there was something vaguely familiar about her, as if I had seen her somewhere. Recently. She had a coffee mug in her hand, a cigarette in her mouth, and a bored look on her face. "What do you want?" she asked.

"What is it that makes you women fall all over me when you first meet me?" I asked. "Charisma?"

"What are you talking about?"

"Maybe it's my looks."

"You don't start making sense," the woman said, "I'm going to shut the door in your face."

I took out my wallet and showed her the license. "My name's Rhineheart," I said. "I'm a private investigator."

She squinted at the license through a stream of smoke. "A private investigator? You putting me on?"

"You Betty Walker?"

"That's the name I still use," she said. "My ex-husband's named Walker."

"If his name's Eddie, he's the one I'm looking for," I said.

She grimaced. "What's he done now?"

"I just want to talk to him," I said.

She nodded and made a brief noise, somewhere between a laugh and a snort. She took the cigarette out of her mouth and flipped it over into the gravel. "You better come on in," she said. I followed her into the trailer, one cramped narrow room with a linoleum floor and a sagging couch and a big twenty-five-inch color TV in the corner that seemed to take up half the room. The set was on, but the sound was turned down to a murmur. It was tuned to a daytime game show whose brightly dressed host was smiling like a moron into the camera. It was one of the shows I had seen on Wednesday. Watching it had made me feel half-lobotomized.

"Have a seat," she said.

I perched on the edge of the couch.

"You want a cup of coffee, or anything?"

I shook my head.

"I knew he'd done something wrong when he came by here yesterday." She gestured with the mug. "I hadn't seen Eddie in over a year. We been divorced for over a year now, you know?"

I didn't know, but I nodded.

"He paid me back the three hundred he's been owing me forever," she said. "Plus he gave me an extra fifty. I asked him where he got the money and he told me not to ask him any questions." She sighed. "Same old Eddie. He said he was leaving town, but he didn't say where he was going. Said he didn't know when he'd be back. I said goodbye and good luck, but what I really meant was good riddance. If I had any sense I could've predicted that someone would come by looking for him." She sighed again. "And the truth is, I don't even want to know what he's done now."

"You have an idea where he was headed?"

She nodded. "He lived for a year in Florida when he

THE QUEEN'S MARE

was a young kid. At a place called Sanibel Island. He always talked about going back there someday."

"Did you know what Eddie's been doing for the past year?"

She shook her head. "Like I said, until yesterday I hadn't seen him for over a year."

"Did you know he was working as a groom on a horse farm?"

"He can't stay away from those horses, can he?"

"You got any idea why he had you listed as his nearest relative on his job application?"

She shrugged. "I guess 'cause he thought of me that way. He didn't have anybody else he could call a relative."

"How did Eddie know your address?"

"Eddie used to live *here*, mister. I been living in this same trailer for the past four years. I want to move, but every time I save enough money to get out of here, something happens. Car breaks down. I get sick and have to have an operation."

"What do you do for a living, Betty?"

"I'm between jobs right now. What I do mostly is hostess and bartend and wait tables. I'm collecting unemployment right now."

"You pretty sure Eddie was headed out of town, huh?"

She shrugged. "All I know is what he said."

"In case he didn't leave, you got any idea where he might be?"

"Not the slightest."

"What about friends?"

She snorted. "Eddie didn't have no friends in the way you mean. He never hung around with nobody. Mostly what he did when he wasn't at home was chase after as many different whores and sluts as he could. When he was home, he got drunk and beat me up." She set the coffee mug down on a scarred little side table. "Eddie's not in my life no more, and I don't like to think about him. Brings back too many bad memories. I didn't want to see him yesterday, and I don't want to talk about him anymore."

I got up and took a card out and handed it to her. It was my day for giving out cards. "If you think of anything that might help me find Eddie, I'd appreciate a call."

I left her peering down at my card with a dubious look on her face.

TWENTY

I needed to go home and go to sleep. It was the middle of the afternoon but I had been up twenty-eight straight hours. My head felt swollen and my eyes were gritty from lack of sleep. I drove back to the office. McGraw was gone. She'd left a note on her desk. "Gone to STAKEOUT/RESEARCH. Three calls: Charlotte Beaumont, Diane Carter, Lucky T. Lucky wants to see you. He wants you to come out to the Downs, to the Skye Terrace (Millionaires Row). He's left a ticket for you at the main clubhouse entrance. The other two want you to call. You private-eye types sure do lead mysterious, exciting, glamorous lives. You get invited a lot of places and folks are always calling. Speaking of that, our landlord called to say that he's had another complaint about us from the restaurant downstairs and we'd better not be late with the rent again or it's eviction time for sure."

I called Charlotte Beaumont first. She was *not*, the desk clerk at the Seelbach informed me in haughty tones, available for any calls. If I would be so kind as to leave my number, he would do his best to see that Ms. Beaumont got my message. Get fucked, is what I felt like telling the jerk, but instead I told him my name and when I mentioned it, the clerk said, "Just a moment, please. I have a message for a Mr. Rhineheart. Ms. Charlotte Beaumont expects you for dinner in her suite at seven o'clock P.M. sharp."

I hung up and dialed Diane Carter's office number next. She answered the phone.

"Michael. Are you all right?"

"I'm okay."

Diane Carter said she was sorry about what had happened this morning. She thought I had been treated unfairly. "I probably should have spoken up, but I don't know what good it would have done." The reason she was calling, she said, was to offer her help. She was pleased that I was going to remain on the case and if there was anything she could do to help...

"How come you didn't tell me about the death threats?"

"How did you find out about the threats? Hattie and I and—Did Shirley or Charlotte tell you?"

"What difference does it make *who* told me? I know about them, and I want to know why you didn't tell me."

"Michael, I was sworn to secrecy. Hattie wanted no one outside the family to know about those calls. She insisted upon secrecy."

"Any idea why?"

"I think her feeling is that any outsider finding out about them would only add to her problems. She wouldn't even tell Mr. Thornton."

"He ever give any indication that he knew about them anyway?"

"No."

"Tell me about the calls. How many where there?"

"Two. The first one was at the beginning of April. The second one was two weeks ago." Basically, the same time as the calls to Shirley. The natural question was whether Charlotte had received a similar pair of calls. I would have to ask her about that.

"Did you hear either call?"

Diane shook her head. "Hattie told me about them. She said the caller was a man with a strange-sounding voice. As if he were speaking in an echo chamber or something. I'm not sure of the exact words of the threat, but according to Hattie it was something on the order of it being time for justice on the Beaumont family for their sins and that Hattie's turn to die was coming soon."

"The caller said 'justice on the Beaumont family for their *sins*'?"

"That's what Hattie said."

"Any idea what that means?"

"No. Hattie didn't either." There was a silence on the other end of the line, then Diane said, "Michael, you don't think there's a chance that these threats are serious, do you?"

"I don't know," I said.

"Michael, I carry a gun in my purse. A .22."

"Do you know how to use it?"

"I fire on a range once a month."

Firing a pistol on a range and being able to shoot someone were as different as fire and ice. "You're probably not going to have to use it, but there's nothing wrong with being ready."

"Hattie has a pistol, too."

Ashtree, it seemed, was an armed camp. "The thing to do," I said, "is stay alert and be prepared." It was advice right out of the *Boy Scout Manual*, but that didn't make it any less true.

"Is there any thing I can do to help you in any way?"

"If there is," I said, "I'll call you."

"Please. Don't hesitate," she said. She gave me her home phone number and her home address, a fashionable high-rise apartment building in the East End.

I said goodbye and hung up. I dug out Eddie Walker's personnel file and double-checked the name of one of his references. James Bergman, an attorney. I made a telephone call to a friend in the Louisville Bar Association. I told her what I was looking for and in a few minutes she provided me with the information I was looking for.

"Thanks, babe."

I hung up and almost immediately the phone began to ring. I picked up the receiver. "Rhineheart here."

"Mr. Rhineheart?"

There was no mistaking the throaty sound of Paige's voice.

"What can I do for you, Paige?"

"I need to talk to you. Privately."

"How come all of a sudden everybody wants to talk to me?"

"It's about the case."

"Where are you?" I asked.

"I'm at school. My last class will be over in twenty-five minutes."

This was my day for seeing people. If the day lasted long enough, and I could hold up, I might get around to see the whole Beaumont family and visit with everyone connected to the case.

"I'll pick you up in front of the place," I said. "Tell me how to get there."

Saint Paul's Episcopal School for Girls was an ivy-covered redbrick edifice whose facade gave off an imposing air of money and tradition and Protestant rectitude. Paige was standing on the sidewalk out front, holding an armful of books. She was dressed in a typical private-school girl's uniform: white blouse, dark skirt, knee stockings, but on Paige the clothes looked like an outfit that belonged in the bedroom.

The blouse, unbuttoned at the neck, was tight and clinging. And the skirt, which embraced her hips as if it had been pasted on, was short enough to be illegal in some jurisdictions. She slid into the car, her skirt hiking up to reveal an expanse of creamy thigh joined to a perfectly dimpled knee. She wriggled about, settling herself in the seat. I pulled away from the curb, making every effort to keep my eyes on the road and my mind off her body. Trying to remember the current minimum sentence for statutory rape was helpful. I pointed the Maverick in the direction of Ashtree.

"I need your advice, Mr. Rhineheart."

Paige fiddled with the strap on her purse. She looked out the window. It was as if she were embarrassed about something, as unlikely as that seemed. When she spoke her voice was hesitant, almost timid. "I've got a confession to make."

"Save it," I said. "I don't want to hear about it."

She turned to me with a shocked look, as if I had just slapped her in the face. I'd told her the truth. I was sick of hearing confessions, tired of listening to other people's problems. I wasn't a priest or a psychiatrist. I had no answers, no real sympathy for their concerns. The last thing I wanted to hear about was the problems of a rich, fifteen-year-old high school girl.

"But don't you help people?" she asked. "I thought ... you were supposed to help people."

"Where is *that* written? I'm a private dick. You pay me to do a thing, and I do it. It's a business," I said.

"I've got money," she said. "I can pay you. I've got my own bank account."

"Save your money," I said. "Tell your problem to your mother."

"My *mother*?"

"Mothers are good with problems," I said, although I wasn't sure that applied to Charlotte Beaumont. "Let her take care of it."

"Oh God," Paige said, "I can't even *talk* to my mother..."

"Tell your grandmother then." I didn't add *she's rich enough to handle whatever it is*.

"I can't," she said. "I can't tell Grandmother this... It's about... Eddie Walker..."

She'd got my attention. "What about Eddie Walker?"

Paige dug something out of her purse and handed it to me. It was a photograph, wallet-sized, a snapshot of

Paige. She was standing next to a bed. She had a can of beer in one hand and what looked like a joint in her mouth. She was naked. If there was any doubt that Paige was a woman from head to toe, the photograph dispelled it.

I gave it back to her. "You've got a nice body, kid." My voice was even and level. Mr. Cool. "Especially for a fifteen-year-old. Why are you showing it to me?"

"This is just a copy," she said. "Eddie has the original."

"Eddie as in Walker?"

She nodded.

"He the photographer?"

She nodded again.

"Is this the only picture?"

She shook her head. "There are two or three more. This is the least..." She searched for a word.

"The least... what?"

"In the others I'm... doing stuff."

Doing stuff. "You and Eddie must have been pretty friendly," I suggested.

She shook her head. "We were never friends. We got it on together a lot, but I don't think we spoke three words to each other the whole time. We didn't have much in common, actually."

We were in the Brownsboro Road area. Outside the window, the landscape was green lawns and shade trees, the architecture was fake Tudor mixed in with long low-slung ranch styles. We were in the midst of middle-class suburban subdivided America.

"What are we talking about here, Paige? Blackmail?"

Paige nodded. "One day last month, Eddie said he wanted some money. He said he would show Grandmother the pictures if I didn't give him money. So I did. I gave him five hundred dollars at first, then more. I gave him over a thousand dollars, all together." Paige paused a moment, I looked over and she was staring out the window. She went on, "He was supposed to give me the photographs when I gave him the money, but he never did. I want to get those photographs, Mr. Rhineheart. Grandmother doesn't know about me... about... all the stuff I do. I don't want her to find out. I don't want her to see those photographs."

"You want *me* to find them," I said.

Paige shrugged. "I guess. This morning you told Grandmother that no matter what, you were going to find the mare and the foal and the money. I thought that maybe while you're searching for Eddie you might come across the photographs." She looked over at me with those big round innocent fifteen-year-old eyes.

"I don't think so," I said. "It doesn't sound like my kind of deal. Besides, I'm going to have my hands full looking for the ransom and the mare and the foal. I doubt I'll have time to be looking for any photographs."

Paige was quiet for a moment, then she said, "If it's a matter of money, I could pay you. I could pay you out of my account, or... any way you wanted me to ... really." She smiled and reached over and put her hand on my thigh.

I looked down at her hand, then over at her, then back up at the road. I was still traveling in a straight line. Relatively. "Paige," I said evenly, "am I going to have to make you sit in the backseat?"

She giggled and removed her hand. "What can I do to get you to help me, Mr. Rhineheart?"

"Quit bullshitting me for one thing," I said.

"I have this counselor," Paige said. "Her name is Ms. Fowler. She says the reason I lie so much is because I don't put enough value on myself. She says that's why I'm so"—Paige hesitated over the word—"*promiscuous*. She says that comes from low self-esteem."

"She may have something there," I said. I waited a beat, then I said, "Paige, why don't you tell me what you had to do with the kidnapping?"

TWENTY-ONE

PAIGE fastened her eyes on mine. Her face was pale. "How—how did you know?"

I shrugged. "I do this stuff for a living, babe."

"Oh God, you can't tell Grandmother. You have to promise not to tell Grandmother, or *anyone*."

"Don't worry," I said. With the exception of Farnsworth and McGraw, who was I going to tell? I didn't trust anyone else.

"You couldn't really say I helped with the kidnapping," Paige said. "I didn't know that a kidnapping was going to take place. Eddie asked me to start a small brushfire in the north pasture that night. He'd cleared the ground and fixed it so that it would burn itself out. All I had to do was light it. He said he was going to play a joke on George Parker, the barn watchman. He said it wouldn't do any harm. I had no idea what it was really for, or else I wouldn't have done it." She looked at me. "You believe me, don't you, Mr. Rhineheart?"

"Sure," I lied. I didn't know if Paige was telling the truth, or not. At this point it didn't seem to make a whole lot of difference. "What did you do after you set the fire?"

"I went back to my room. I was high. I'd done some grass earlier, and I went to sleep. The next day is when I found out about the kidnapping. I didn't know what to do. I realized that I had played some part in it. I was scared. I went to Eddie. He denied knowing anything about the kidnapping. He said the fire and the theft weren't connected. He said if I told anyone about setting the fire he would tell everyone the whole thing was my idea and give the pictures to my grandmother. Then the next day he was gone. I didn't know what to do, Mr. Rhineheart. You're the first person I've told." She turned her big dark eyes on me. "I didn't have anyone else to turn to."

It was a heart-melting performance. It made you want to take her in your arms and comfort her. But that wasn't the way to deal with Paige. "I'm getting ready to shed a tear here," I said.

Paige looked at me with disbelief, then she giggled. "Oh God, you're so... *mean*."

"I'm not mean," I said. "I just say what I think. And if you want me to find those photographs, you're going to have to stop bullshitting around and help me."

"Will you look for them, then?"

"I'll give it a shot," I said. "But I need your help to find Walker. I want you to tell me everything you know about him that might help me locate him."

"I'll try," she said. "The trouble is I don't know much about him. I don't know anything *personal* about him."

I looked at Paige to see if she was being sarcastic, but her face was as bland and as innocent as any tenth grader's. She saw no irony in not knowing anything personal about someone she'd "got it on with a lot."

We passed the Holiday Manor shopping center and turned onto U.S. 42. Ashtree was just a few miles down the road. As we drove Paige told me what she knew about Walker.

He smoked Camel filters and drank beer. He took dope whenever he got a chance, pills, pot, whatever, sometimes when he was on the job, but most often not. He was from around Louisville and had grown up in an orphanage in the area. He said he'd been in the navy. He told her about all the ports he'd visited. He said he'd been in prison for something. When he first told her she hadn't believed him, but now she wasn't so sure.

Walker was the silent type. He didn't talk much and was secretive and suspicious of everyone. He didn't like any of the people he worked with. He said he was working as a groom so he could learn about horses and become a trainer.

Walker was in his thirties and the oldest guy she'd ever been to bed with. He was over six feet tall, had a lot of muscles, and a really sexy way about him. They'd "got it on" in the guard cubicle, and in the breeding barns, and once late at night he had come to her room. Most of the time though they went to his apartment, which wasn't much of a place, but at least had a bed. Paige said she didn't know all the reasons why she had sex with Walker. Maybe it was the reason she had sex with a lot of different boys. Maybe it had something to do with low self-esteem and maybe it didn't. Maybe she just wanted to have fun. Or maybe she was trying to get back at her mother, who in some ways was a real bitch, or her father, whom she hadn't seen since she was three. Anyway, what was the difference.

Walker did a lot of bragging about all of his women. He said he'd had dozens of girlfriends. He'd been married once. To a woman named Betty who lived in a trailer park over around Dixie Highway.

Whoa. "How do you know that?"

"That he'd been married? He told me."

"How do you know she lives in a trailer park near Dixie Highway?"

"I went with him one time when he went to see her."

"When was this?"

"Last month some time. He wouldn't let me meet her. I had to sit in the car and wait until he came out." She looked at me. "Is that important?"

"It might be," I said. It meant that Betty Walker had been lying when she said she hadn't seen Eddie in over a year. The natural question that followed was what else had she been lying about.

"Tell me something," I said to Paige, "did anyone ever come out to the farm and visit Eddie?"

"I don't think so," she said.

"Tell me more about him," I said, as we turned into the main farm entrance. The guard on duty in the cubicle was a dark-haired young man in a sharply pressed uniform. He waved at Paige who smiled and fluttered her fingers in a familiar gesture in return.

Paige said she didn't know what else there was to tell. Once Eddie had taken her over to a honky-tonk bar near the Louisville stockyards. It was a wild place filled with motorcycle types and people like that. They hadn't even carded her.

I asked her if the people there seemed to know Walter.

Paige shook her head. "I don't think so." Paige put her hand on my arm. "I just remembered something. You asked if anyone ever came out to the farm to see Eddie. Well, a couple of months ago, someone came out to see him. It just happened once but I remember it because Eddie seemed different after this guy visited him."

"What do you mean *different*?"

"I don't know exactly. Different. Nervous. On edge. Something."

"Tell me about the visitor."

"He had light brown hair and wore thick glasses."

"How old was he?"

She shrugged. "Around Eddie's age, I guess."

We pulled up the driveway and stopped in front of the house. Paige gathered up her books.

"Anything else?"

"Not that I can remember."

"What kind of car did the visitor drive?"

"He didn't. He drove a truck."

I looked over at Paige, who had pushed down on the

door handle and was getting out of the car. "What kind of truck?"

"A, you know, pickup."

"What color?"

"Huh?"

"What color was the truck?"

"Red."

Bingo. Sometimes, if you kept poking around long enough, you bumped into something important, something that connected to something else.

Paige was half in, half out of the car.

"You remember anything else about the truck? The make? The license number?"

Paige shook her head. "Who remembers trucks?"

"Was it Japanese?"

"I don't know." She pointed to one of the front windows. "Someone is watching us from the window." I looked where she pointed, but saw nothing. I got a card out of my pocket and held it out to her. It was the same card I'd given to Shirley Beaumont and to Betty Walker and earlier to Paige's mother, Charlotte. "You remember anything else that might help, give me a call."

She smiled and took the card. "I hear you met my mother the other day," she said. "What do you think of her?"

"She's very attractive," I said.

Paige did something with her eyebrows. "She thinks you're hot shit, too. Are you going to sleep with her?"

I didn't reply. I nodded at her books. "You better get in and do your homework," I said.

Paige slid the rest of the way out of the car and slammed the door angrily. She turned without saying goodbye and strode off toward the house. Halfway there, she turned around, shifted her books from one arm to the other, smiled a wicked smile, and gave me the finger.

TWENTY-TWO

I drove back to the city thinking about the case. All in all, it had been a fair day. I had lost a client but had gained some important pieces of information. One: It was clear that Walker had been involved in the theft of the mare and the foal. Two: a man who had visited Walker drove a red pickup similar to the one Farns had seen leaving the riding stables. And three: Betty Walker had lied to me about the last time she had seen Eddie. Did that mean the rest of what she'd told me was untrue? Maybe. Maybe Eddie Walker hadn't left town at all and was hiding. Which brought up the possibility of staking out her trailer. With Farns already watching Graves, and McGraw on Thornton, it wouldn't be possible to do any kind of serious around-the-clock surveillance job.

I'd have to put together some kind of hit-and-miss operation, which was a fairly accurate description of the way things were already going, but better than nothing. If I had to, I could have McGraw drop Thornton and pick up Betty Walker. That would probably piss off McGraw, who didn't like stakeouts to begin with. The thought of an angry McGraw cheered me up a little, and I hit the gas and whipped the car in and out of traffic as if it wasn't fourteen years old and didn't have a bad rear end. I wanted to get back out to Dixie Highway to set the stakeout on Betty in motion, but I had to make a couple of stops on the way.

LT's place was first.

Fat, forty, an unkempt bachelor who lived with his mother in a frame bungalow on S. Jackson Street, LT was my connection to the world of computers. A postal clerk, LT worked the midnight shift at the downtown P.O. and spent his entire salary on computers and software and related items. He passed his days in his basement surrounded by his equipment, building computers, devising and installing systems, analyzing programs, programming, "hacking," doing whatever it was that computer maniacs did. As far as I knew, LT never slept.

When I rang the bell at LT's house, his mother opened the door. She had a rosary wrapped around her fingers. She gave me a martyr's smile, one that said she was doing her best in the face of having a strange son who got visits from sleazy characters like me, and without a word of greeting pointed me down the stairs.

The basement was a maze of computer equipment: six or seven CRTs, half a dozen keyboards, four printers, two of which were clacking out data on long rolls of computer paper. The green and yellow screens contained rows of words and numbers. Some had graphs and mathematical symbols. $82F = W7 = >8]F?$ $XWWIFP7\ D]S:WXD(Vp6w6n?$ There were tractor feeders and cut-sheet feeders and modems and boxes full of disks, and strung about the basement ceiling and across the floor were enough wires, cables, plugs, surge protectors, and power boards to stock an electric power station.

LT was seated in front of a keyboard, his fingers flying across the keys as he talked into a phone that was attached to his head like a set of earphones. He didn't notice me for a few moments, but he looked up finally, and when he saw me, his broad face broke into a childlike smile.

He said, "Hey, Rhineheart, how's it going, man? What's happening in the private-eye world?"

"Same old stuff," I said. "What have you been up to?"

He took off the headset, but continued to key while we talked. "Oh, man," he said, rolling his eyes upward, "I been doing a lot of messing around. Two weeks ago I penetrated the state police computer, and then last week I got into the FBI."

"What do you mean *you got into the FBI*?"

"I mean I got *in there*, Rhine. I penetrated their system, man. With a modem and my trusty little Sanyo."

"What did you do when you went in there, LT?"

"I looked around, checked them out, copied a couple of files, got back out."

"LT, you *are* talking about the local FBI, aren't you?"

He smiled widely and shook his head. "I'm talking about D.C. man. I'm talking the J. Edgar Hoover Building on I-forget-the-name-of-the-street."

"You better watch yourself, LT. The Feds don't like nobody messing with their files."

"Fuck 'em is what I say," LT said, "if they can't take a joke."

"I need some help, LT."

But LT wasn't listening. He was still keying away and he had a rapt, bemused look on his face. "You know where I'm going to strike next, Rhine?"

"Huh?"

"Next I'm going after the CIA."

"That might not be a good move, LT."

"Langley, Virginia, is where they're located, Rhine."

"That's what I heard, LT." I cleared my throat. "LT, I need your help."

"Say the word, bro."

"I need to find out if a guy named Eddie Walker has a police record?"

"You got his social security number, Rhine?"

"Yeah." I read it to him off Walker's record.

LT copied it down. "He's ours."

"Plus I need to track down a pickup truck."

"If it's been registered somewhere and it's on a computer, it's ours, too." His fingers paused over the keys. He picked up a pencil. "What's that social security number?"

I gave it to him.

"What kind of data you got on the vehicle?" LT pronounced it *Vee*-hicle.

"I don't have the license plate. Is that going to do us in?"

"Not necessarily," LT said. "You know what year it was made?"

"Late. Last year or this year."

"What make?"

"Toyota."

He shook his head. "Them fucking Japs. They're gonna own the U.S. of A. one day, Rhine."

"It's red."

"Color's helpful," he said. Then he frowned. "I think..." He chewed on the pencil stub. "I think color's on the registration."

"Kentucky plates," I said. "Probably Jefferson County, or something close."

"Jefferson, Oldham, Bullitt, Shelby, Meade, Hardin?"

"Sounds good."

"Lets throw in Anderson," LT said.

"I need to find out how many red Toyota pickups and who owns them. Names and addresses of the owners."

"You got it," LT said. "Top priority."

"How long will this take?"

LT knitted his brow thoughtfully. "A week?"

"I don't have a week."

"Three days then."

"Can you do it any sooner than that?"

LT shrugged. "I can try, bro."

THE QUEEN'S MARE

"What about the information on Walker?"

"That'll be a lot faster. Tonight or tomorrow."

"You call me when you get it, LT?"

"The very minute."

"One other thing," I said. "If I wanted you to find out who owned a particular piece of property, say in Bullitt County—how long would that take?"

LT smiled. "Thirty seconds. I got the State Property Tax records in my files."

"Can you pull up who owns the Bullitt County Riding Stable property on Highway 6, outside Shepherdsville?"

LT's fingers danced over the keys. A half a minute later he beckoned me over to the screen.

STATE OF KENTUCKY
PROPERTY VALUATION DEPARTMENT
Property: Bullitt County Riding Stables.
Size: 4.3 acres
Structures: 2 buildings (office, barn), riding ring
Estimated value: $80,000
Owner: Central Kentucky Real Estate Investment Corp.
President, Wallace Thornton.

"Thanks, LT." I made to leave.

"Hey, Rhine. Guess where I strike after I do the CIA?"

I was afraid to guess. "Where, LT?"

"IRS, man. Treasury department. Got the address somewhere. Going in there. Don't exactly know what I'm going to do when I get in. Gonna do something though. Copy some programs. Might erase some records. Shit, might erase *all* the motherfucking records. Have to see when I get there." He smiled. "Blow some smoke up their revenue-collecting ass." LT held up a finger. "But don't worry, I'll find the guy and the red pickup first. You got priority, Rhine."

"Thanks, LT."

"Take it easy, Rhine."

TWENTY-THREE

My next stop was the Downs. It was almost five when I parked in the main clubhouse lot. I picked up my pass at the gate, made my way across the bricks and took the elevator up to the Skye Terrace. When I stepped off the elevator, the first thing that caught my eye was a banner proclaiming *Lucky Thompson Day at the Downs*. It was strung from the ceiling above rows of linen-covered tables, which were crowded with a variety of folk: local celebrities, politicians, racing officials, media people, high rollers, and numbers of ordinary partygoers and celebrants. Everyone was well and expensively dressed. All the women looked good. A couple of them were striking.

A gray-haired maître d' standing behind a podium gave my jeans, sport coat, and open-necked shirt a bad look. Obviously, I wasn't his idea of a high roller. I showed him my pass. He frowned at it, then showed me some teeth, and said, "Follow me." He led me to a small table near the front of the room, where Lucky Thompson was seated alone. Lucky was wearing an Irish walking hat and an expensive-looking light-colored suit. His wrinkled leathery face wore the same look as it did on TV when he was explaining to folks why he was the best horse trainer in the world. I looked down at his little feet. They were encased in a pair of lizard-skin boots. He pointed a finger at me. "Last time I seen you was at the stockholders' party."

THE QUEEN'S MARE

"What did you want to see me about?" I said.

"How'd you like that girl I was at the party with?"

"Way too young for you, and for a high-priced hooker, a real dog."

"You come on pretty strong, Mr. Detective. You as bad as you act?"

"I'm worse," I said.

Lucky smiled. He liked that. "Have a seat, Mr. Detective. Let's you and me have a little chitchat. Won't take but a few minutes, but it'll be worth your time."

I sat down and as I lowered myself into a chair I noticed Thompson glance at the adjoining table. It was occupied by a man so large he looked as if he belonged to a different species. The man had huge shoulders, a massive chest, and thick hairy arms. He was wearing tent-sized clothes, a polo shirt, beige slacks, size 18 triple E brogans. His head was oversized and covered with lank brown hair that hung down to his shoulders.

I pegged Mr. Mammoth at six-eight, three hundred and fifty pounds, but he was sitting down, and he might have been bigger than that. He looked big enough to blot out the sun. His size, however, wasn't the scariest thing about him. The scary thing was his thickly featured face, which was as blank and raw and mindless as a slab of meat.

To Thompson, I said, "You going to introduce me to your friend?"

Lucky's laugh was a harsh little he-he-he sound. "You're observant," he said. "But no, I'm not going to introduce you. That's Ruben, my bodyguard. I don't introduce him to nobody. Ruben don't socialize. He ain't got brain one. He don't know how to talk to people for one thing. He got no social graces for another. He's like a goddamn animal. I keep him on my payroll 'cause he does his job."

"What do you need a bodyguard for?" I asked.

"Oh, I got a host of enemies, friend. A veritable host. Fame's not what it's cracked up to be, son. It brings a lot of bad people into your life. All of 'em want a piece of you. There's some that want to do violence to my person. I pay Ruben here to see that that doesn't happen." Thompson looked at his watch and frowned. "But I ain't got time to be bullshitting with you about this. They going to do a prime-time interview with me in about ten minutes over in the Director's Room, and I need to be finished up, so I can concentrate on that." He cleared his throat. "Let's talk bidness. How much?"

In the few minutes we'd been talking, he'd managed to irritate me a half dozen different ways. "What the hell are you talking about?" I asked.

"How much you want to give me the whole rundown on what's been going on at Ashtree? I'm talking the complete story from beginning to end, including what happened last night and this morning. I hear you fucked up and got fired and that the mare and the foal are out there somewhere. But I don't know if that's gospel truth or a bunch of horseshit. I got a number of different sources telling me this and that, but I need to verify it. You the only one knows for sure, so obviously you're the one to come to. I'm big on verification. That's how I am, son. I follow through on things, go to the little extra expense to make sure I got the right information. It's why I'm number one in my field. Follow up and verify. It's the secret to success in any endeavor. So how much?"

"Let me get this straight," I said. "You want to pay me some money to tell you confidential information about a client?"

Thompson smiled. "*Confidential*'s good. Makes you sound like a professional person, lawyer or accountant or something. But yeah, that's it. I want the whole story. Don't worry though, I'll pay good money for it. Top dollar." He jabbed his hand into his pocket. "How much?"

"What if I said five thousand dollars?"

"Then ah'd say that was way too much." He pulled

THE QUEEN'S MARE

out a thick roll of bills encircled by a silver money clip. "But I'll give you four hundred right now out front without even knowing what kind of information it is. Favorable or unfavorable." He peeled four one-hundred-dollar bills off his roll, made a little fan out of them, and held it out to me.

"Why," I asked, "is this information so important to you?"

Thompson frowned. "Son, you getting your roles mixed up. *Ah'm* the one after the information."

"I got a deal for you," I said. "You tell me about this group of New York investors that wants to take over Ashtree, and I'll tell you what you want to know."

Lucky sighed and returned the bills to his clip, the clip to his pocket. "Son, you fucking with me. I don't appreciate that. I thought we might be able to do a little bidness, but it looks like you want to play a different game. The thang I don't understand is *why*. You trying to prolong this, so I'll come up with more money? Don't outsmart yourself. That information's only worth so much and no more."

I took out the piece of notepaper I had found in Eddie Walker's garbage bag. "I got a note here from you to Eddie Walker, the groom at Ashtree who's disappeared. It says you want to talk to him some more about something you apparently already discussed."

"Where did you get that?"

"I found it."

Lucky held out his hand. "Let me see that."

I shook my head. "What did you want to talk to Eddie about, Lucky? Did it have anything to do with the kidnapping?"

"If you know what's good for you, you'll hand over that note. I can make it hard for you, son." He looked over at Ruben, who began to eye me. I felt like the ant must have felt when he saw the first anteater.

I put the note back in my pocket and stood up. "You're going to be late for your interview, Lucky."

Lucky shook his finger at me. "We'll see each other again," he promised. "Me and you and Ruben."

I gave Ruben a mean look that he didn't even notice, turned, and walked over to the elevator. There was a ticket window close by and before the elevator arrived I bought a ten-dollar ticket on the numbers three and eight in the last race exacta. Thirty-eight. My age.

TWENTY-FOUR

From the Downs I took Third Street to the Watterson, the Watterson to Dixie Highway. Betty Walker's yellow Chevette was still standing in the same spot. I parked alongside a dumpster down the road from the trailer. The Maverick was partially hidden, but I had a clear view of the trailer.

I got out of the car and strolled around the corner to the trailer park office, a squat concrete block building. There were two outdoor phones. I used one to make a quick call to the office. The answering service operator picked up the phone, which meant that McGraw was not there. I identified myself, and was given the message that Farnsworth had called and would call back later and that McGraw had called and could be reached at home. I thanked the woman, hung up, and dialed McGraw's home number.

When she answered, I said, "What are you doing at home?"

"I'm resting up," she said. "I spent four hours watching Thornton's office and nothing makes me more tired than that kind of stuff."

"He have any significant visitors?"

"Shirley Beaumont. I recognized her from the newspaper photograph."

I made a little humming sound, like Basil Rathbone in *The Hound of the Baskervilles*.

"I went to see the insurance guy, Dixon," McGraw

said. "Told him I was an investigator for the State Insurance Commission. He didn't even ask for I.D. He told me he wrote a six-million-dollar theft policy on Winterset three months ago. Hattie is beneficiary."

I digested that in silence.

"As soon as I get a shower," McGraw said, "I'm going over and stake out his house. He lives in Indian Hills."

"Belay that," I said. "We'll have to drop Thornton for the time being. We don't have enough manpower, or maybe I should say *personpower*."

"Funny."

"I got somebody more important for you to watch. Betty Walker. Eddie's ex. She lives in a trailer in the Valley Station Mobile Home Park. Lot 26, H Street. I need you to come out and spell me for a while."

McGraw made a moaning sound.

"What kind of a noise is that?"

"What does it sound like?" McGraw said. "It's a moan. I *hate* stakeouts. Stakeouts suck. How come you always call on me when it's some kind of deadly boring piece-of-shit job? You never want me to come along when something exciting's going down, like a ransom exchange or a shoot-out."

"What are you talking about? Who gets into shoot-outs?"

"You do. You and Farnsworth do."

"Once or twice is all."

"You know why I never get to do the exciting things?"

"No, but I bet you're going to tell me."

"You're goddamn right I am."

"Wait a minute. Let me guess. You never get to do the exciting things because you're a woman."

"Exactly. Precisely."

"How come I knew that?"

"Because I told you, you shithead."

I gave McGraw directions to the trailer park, told

her where I'd be parked, and said, "I'll see you in half an hour, babe."

"Don't hold your breath," McGraw said. But she was there in thirty-two minutes, pulling her twenty-year-old Volkswagen in next to the Maverick. Next to each other, our cars looked like entries in a "beat-up old car" contest.

McGraw got out and came over to the driver's window.

I pointed out Betty Walker's trailer.

"What does she look like?" McGraw asked.

I described Betty.

"What do you mean 'nice ass'? What kind of a description is 'nice ass'?"

"I'm tired," I said, "and a little bit punchy. Never mind 'nice ass.' Light-brown hair, five-five..."

"Why are we staking *her* out?"

"She lied to me."

"That doesn't seem like a good enough reason."

"It'll have to do," I said. "I'll be back in three or four hours. She makes a move out of the trailer, you stick with her. Remember what I told you about tailing someone on your own?"

"Six car lengths back. Try to keep a vehicle between you and the subject."

"That's right."

"Where you going anyway?"

"I got a couple of important things to do," I said, started up the Maverick, and drove straight downtown to the Seelbach Hotel. It was 6:56 when I pulled up in front. I jumped out of the car and tossed the keys to the doorman, who was wearing a top hat and tails. "Park it carefully," I said.

"Yessir," he said, keeping a straight face.

I strolled into the place, crossed the lobby, and caught an elevator to the fourteenth floor. It was one minute to seven when I knocked on the door to 1407.

Charlotte Beaumont opened the door. She was wearing a simple off-the-shoulder dress with straps, but she looked like a million dollars.

"You're going to have to excuse how I'm dressed," I said. "I didn't have time to put on a tie."

"I don't care how you're dressed," Charlotte said. "I'm not interested in your clothes." She gave a smoldering look.

"You look very nice," I said.

"I'm not wearing anything under this dress," she said.

I took a deep breath. "I thought *I* was the one who didn't waste any time."

"Are you going to kiss me, or what?"

I took her in my arms and kissed her. Her mouth opened under mine and with a simple shrug of her shoulders the dress dropped to the floor. I kicked the door shut behind me and we followed the dress to the carpet. We didn't make it out of the foyer for another hour.

When we did it was to move into the bedroom, where we spent another two hours. Charlotte had an electronic alarm clock on a table next to her bed, and when I finally took the opportunity to sit up and take a look at it, it read 10:36. I was starving. "I thought we were going to have dinner," I said, rubbing my stomach. "I'm a little hungry."

"Hungry?" Charlotte gave me an amused look. She reached over and pulled me down on top of her. Some time later I raised up and looked at the clock again. It was 12:01.

"You like White Castles?" I asked Charlotte.

"You keep talking about *food*," she said.

"It's just that I haven't eaten all day," I said, "and I've got this feeling that I'm probably going to need a little something to restore my energy here."

Charlotte giggled. "You're probably right about that." She held up three fingers. "I'll take three with mustard, some fries, and a large Coke."

I threw on my clothes, took the elevator down to the

parking garage, jumped in the Maverick and drove over to the White Castle at Seventh and Broadway, where I got Charlotte's order, plus six, a large fries, and a Coke for myself. We ate them in bed while Charlotte tried to pump me about the case.

"Mama fired you, huh?"

"More or less."

"Did she fire you, or not?"

"Pretty much."

"Paige tells me you're going to stay on the case, however."

"I might."

"So what all have you learned, Michael?"

"About what?"

"About the case."

"Not much."

"Who do you think was responsible for the kidnapping?"

"No idea."

"I understand that you think that the farm worker who disappeared had something to do with it?"

"He might have. On the other hand . . ." I shrugged.

"What about Wallace?"

"What about him?"

"You think there's a possibility he had something to do with it?"

"Maybe."

"Any evidence on him?"

"Not really."

"You do know that Mama took out a big theft insurance policy on Winterset with John Dixon earlier this year?"

"No," I said. On a case, when it came to lying I was like everyone else and lied even when I didn't need to. Why not?

"Of course," she said, "it was right after that European horse got kidnapped . . . but still . . ." She was silent a moment, then she said, "You know who I would be investigating, if *I* were doing the investigating?"

"Who?"

"Sister Shirley."

"How come?"

"A number of reasons," Charlotte said, with an indignant toss of her head. "She has absolutely no loyalty to the family. She takes the family money and gives it to all her lesbian friends through that society she formulated. She doesn't care about Ashtree or Mama or me or the Beaumont family name. If she did she wouldn't be carrying on with her conspicuous lesbian activity in public. You would think that as a Beaumont she would have the grace to keep her sexual preferences in the closet where they belong."

"You know anything about Shirley's business investments?"

"Just that they've all been failures," Charlotte said. "She deludes herself into believing she's the Great American Businesswoman, but I hear she's losing money hand over fist. Gossip has it that she's even in debt to some criminal person here in Louisville. You know anything about that, Michael?"

I shook my head and took a bite of my burger.

"You get any death threats lately, Charlotte?"

"Two. They said basically the same things that Mama's and Shirley's did."

"Didn't they frighten you?"

Charlotte gave me a look. "The only thing that frightens me, Michael, is the possibility that I might not live my life to the fullest." She set her cup on the table. "Hurry up with your food," she said, her eyes gleaming.

Afterwards, I dropped off to sleep and when I opened my eyes it was 8:15 A.M. on Friday morning.

TWENTY-FIVE

On the what-the-hell,-another-hour-probably-won't-make-it-any-worse principle, I woke up Charlotte, told her I was leaving—she barely stirred—got dressed, drove home, took a shower, shaved and changed clothes. When I pulled up to the trailer park dumpster, it was 9:35 by my watch.

I walked over and McGraw rolled down her window. The look she gave me was both bleary-eyed and accusing. "You said four hours," she said between tight lips.

"I made a mistake," I said. "Are you awake enough to drive home?"

"What about an 'I'm sorry'?"

"I'm sorry, McGraw."

"I took some bifetamine around two in the morning," McGraw said. "I only hope I can go to sleep."

"Take the day off," I said. "Sleep as late as you want. But before you go to bed, call Farnsworth and tell him to try to get in touch with me today."

McGraw nodded. "She went out around ten last night. To the convenience store. She bought some groceries and when she came out she used the outdoor phone. She made two calls. First one was short, less than a minute. The second was five or six minutes, and I think it was long distance. She put two or three quarters in the slot."

Long distance, but three or four quarters was local . . . one of the surrounding counties . . . maybe.

"She didn't spot you?" I asked.

"Not a chance," McGraw said.

"Good girl," I said.

She gave me a bad look.

"Good *person*?"

"I'm going home," McGraw said, and started up her car.

"You did a good job," I said.

"Thanks," she said, and drove off.

I got back in my car and flipped on the radio, which was tuned to the local jazz station. At this time of the day the station carried news programs. I sat there listening to reports from different areas of the world. As usual things were bad all over.

It was a few minutes past 11:00 A.M. and I was listening to an analysis of the Third World debt problem when the front door of the trailer opened and Betty Walker came bopping down the steps.

She was dressed in a skirt and jacket and her sandy-colored hair was pulled back from her face and pinned up. She wore large framed designer glasses. She got into the Chevette, backed it out onto the gravel, and pulled off. I waited a minute, then followed. The Chevette wound its way through the maze of trailer park streets to the main entrance where it turned right toward Dixie Highway. At Dixie Betty made a left, heading north toward the city. I tried to stay fifty yards behind her.

She turned onto the eastbound ramp of the Watterson Expressway and took it all the way over to the Middletown exit, easing the Chevette into the middle lane of southbound traffic on Shelbyville Road. A few blocks past the Oxmoor Shopping Center, she grabbed a right and followed a winding residential road a half mile before she turned into the driveway of a single-story U-shaped redbrick building that had the unmistakable air of a nursing home or a hospital. A sign on the neatly trimmed front lawn read OXMOOR MANOR.

As I cruised past the place, I saw that she had parked the Chevette in a paved parking area on that side of the building and was crossing the lot toward an entrance. On the far side of the building an open area of garden paths and green grass and well-tended shrubbery extended across an acre or so of ground to the edge of a small woods. The landscape was dotted with large oak trees and scattered about the grounds were benches and seats occupied by people of various ages. There were some people on the paths: two small boys, an old gentleman with a cane, and a heavy woman wearing a flowing print dress.

I took the Maverick down to the end of the street, turned around, and parked halfway down the block. I had a pair of binoculars in the glove compartment, and when Betty came out of a side entrance about ten minutes later, I trained them on her. She was pushing someone, a brown-haired man wearing a bathrobe—in a wheelchair. I focused the glasses on the man's face. It was round, but pinched-looking. There was a vacant look in the man's eyes, and something recognizable about his face. I had seen it or faces like it before.

For the next half hour I watched Betty Walker push the man in the wheelchair around the grounds. Whenever I put the binoculars on them, she was doing the talking. The man just sat there in the chair looking out of it. As far as I could tell, he never said a word. Then it dawned on me. He was retarded and the look I had seen on his face was that special look of the mentally retarded.

I put the glasses on the woman in the print dress. She had the same look. So did the two young boys. Which meant the place was probably some kind of institution for the retarded.

Eventually, Betty Walker wheeled the man back into the building. I sat tight and in fifteen minutes the Chevette came nosing down the drive and turned right, headed back toward Shelbyville Road. I started the Maverick and followed. I had an idea she was returning to the trailer park, but I was wrong. She got back on the expressway headed west, but took a right on I-64 and rode it all the way into the city, exiting at the Downtown Louisville—Third Street ramp.

She drove the Chevette down Third Street to Main, and along Main to Sixth. She turned left at Sixth and just past Jefferson she swung into a parking garage that adjoined Professional Towers, the building that housed Wallace Thornton's law office. I wheeled the Maverick into a NO PARKING area in front of the building and shut off the engine. I got out and went around to the front of the car and raised the hood. It wasn't the slickest ruse ever invented, but maybe it would keep someone from towing it away for fifteen minutes.

I went in the front entrance and walked across the lobby to the bank of elevators. I took one to Thornton's floor, the eleventh. Thornton's office door faced the elevators and was located in the middle of a long carpeted corridor. At both ends of the corridor were exit doors that led to the stairway. I walked down to one, opened it, and stepped into the stairwell. The door even had a small rectangular plastic window in it. Convenient. There was a chance that Betty Walker had pulled into the parking garage next to Thornton's office by coincidence, and I was up here watching and waiting for nothing, but not much of a chance.

Fifteen minutes later, however, when she had not appeared, I was not so sure. I waited five more minutes, then took off down the stairs. Three flights down I came upon a door that exited out onto the top floor of the parking garage. I took it and stepped out onto the garage floor, a wide concrete ramp lined on both sides by cars. EXIT signs and wide white arrows in the concrete pointed the way down the ramp. There must have been fifty cars on this floor alone, and seven more floors below. There was no way. The odds of my running into the Chevette were six million to one, but down was the way I was headed anyway so I started jogging along the ramp. As I turned the curve which led down to the next floor, I spotted the Chevette backing out of a parking space. It was fifty yards away from me and as it quickly braked and headed down the ramp, I realized that there was no way I could catch it.

It had taken me less than two hours to lose her. I was some detective. Farns would be proud as hell of me. The really hard thing was that McGraw had watched Betty Walker all night, had followed her to two separate locations and had stayed right with her. My only hope was that I could somehow keep the fact that I had lost Walker's ex-wife from McGraw. But I doubted it. You couldn't hide much from McGraw.

Off to my right was a sign that said ELEVATORS and I started to walk that way when I noticed another vehicle back out from the same area where the Chevette had been parked. It was a gray-and-black van with whitewalls and mud flaps. There was some silver lettering on the door. I was too far away to make it out, but I already knew what it said. Betty Walker had met with someone from Ashtree Farms. The question *who?* began echoing in my head as I stood there and watched the van drive off and disappear around the next curve.

TWENTY-SIX

THE Maverick was sitting in the same spot with the hood up. No crowd had gathered to look at the exposed six-cylinder two-fifty horsepower engine. I wasn't surprised. I put the hood down, got in and started it up, and pulled it into the lot across the street. Betty Walker was probably headed back to the trailer park, and if so, that was fine, but I didn't see a lot of point in rushing back there. It seemed like a better idea, while I was right here, to go pay a visit to Wallace Thornton.

Thornton's secretary, a heavily made-up redhead, announced my presence over the intercom, then ushered me into his office. Thornton looked as grim as ever. He wore a dark pin-stripe suit and sat stiffly behind his desk. He did not greet me. With the tips of his fingers he pushed a check across the desk.

"At Hattie's request, I've included an extra day's salary on your check. Considering the other night's debacle, I'm sure you'll find it more than sufficient, Mr. Rhineheart. Perhaps embarrassingly so."

I made no move to pick up the check. Unasked, I sat down in the large leather chair facing his desk. "I'd like to ask you a few questions first, Counselor, if you don't mind."

"Of course I mind. You have been dismissed, Mr. Rhineheart. Terminated. You are no longer employed by Ashtree Farms or the Beaumont family. You seem to have a problem with knowing when to quit."

"Actually," I lied, "I've been rehired."

"Rehired? By whom?"

"By a member of the family and a principal shareholder in Ashtree."

"You're joking? Surely."

"I'm afraid not, Counselor."

"Are you talking about one of the girls?"

"My client's identity," I said, "is confidential."

Thornton snorted. "This is ridiculous. Pick up your check and leave, please."

I didn't move.

Thornton reached for the phone. "I can call security and have you forcibly removed."

"Call them," I said. "Call the police if you like."

"I don't think you quite realize your position, Mr. Rhineheart. It would be a mistake to annoy me. I know a great many people. I am a man of some influence in this community. I have friends, for example, who sit on the commission that passes on investigator's licenses."

The old "friends in high places" routine. I'd heard it before. "I'm not impressed by that kind of shit," I said.

"What would you do without a private investigator's license, Mr. Rhineheart? Be a security guard? Work in a factory? Turn to crime?"

"Maybe, or maybe I'd become a lawyer. The truth is I'd do what I do with a license or without one. The thing I don't understand," I added, "is why you're not cooperating with me. Is it because you have something to hide?"

He took his hand away from the phone. "Don't be ridiculous. What would I have to hide?"

I shrugged. "For one thing, you own the riding stable property where the ransom exchange didn't come off."

Thornton coughed into his fist. "Mr. Rhineheart, let's be clear about something. Regardless of who may have hired you, you have, in my view, no official standing whatsoever. If I respond to your questions, it will strictly be voluntary."

When I didn't reply he continued, "I didn't mention being a part-owner of the particular piece of property where the rendezvous took place because I didn't feel that what was entirely coincidental was particularly relevant to the matter at hand, which was the bungled ransom exchange."

"You think that the ransom site being a piece of your property was strictly coincidental?"

"What else could it be?"

"Maybe it was planned. Maybe the thieves wanted to throw some suspicion on you."

Thornton raised an eyebrow. "That hadn't occurred to me. Perhaps you're right."

"On the other hand," I said, "maybe it *was* a coincidence. In my business you run into a lot of coincidences. Take your relationship to Eddie Walker as an example. That's a hell of a coincidence, isn't it?"

Thornton didn't blink. "What are you talking about?"

"Eddie Walker *was* your client once, wasn't he?"

"No," Thornton said with some force, "he was most certainly *not* my client."

"That's pretty emphatic for someone who's just being technical," I said. "He was a client of your firm, one of the junior partners... Bergman."

"How did you find that out?"

"It was no big deal," I said. "A matter of public record. When I saw an attorney listed as a reference on Eddie's job application for Ashtree Farms I had him checked out and found out he worked for you."

"James Bergman was a junior partner of the firm. He is someone I barely know, as a matter of fact. He represented Eddie Walker in a criminal matter. Walker was convicted and served his sentence. He was a model prisoner and was released, as I understand it, on parole with time off for good behavior. Mr. Bergman, who is no longer with the firm, apparently felt that Walker had been rehabilitated, which, I presume, is why he allowed his name to be used as a reference. I don't deal with the criminal end of the firm's business, Mr. Rhineheart, and as far as I know, I have never exchanged a word with Walker. That hardly constitutes a 'relationship.'"

"And yet you seem to know a good deal about his case."

"What are you trying to imply, Mr. Rhineheart?"

I shrugged. "I'm not trying to imply anything. I'm trying to find out whatever I can. There's an apparent connection between you and Eddie Walker. I want to see where that leads."

"It leads nowhere, Mr. Rhineheart. I can assure you of that." He stood up. "Now, if you'll excuse me, I'm a busy man."

"Just a couple more questions, Counselor."

Thornton folded his arms across his chest.

"How come you didn't tell me about the death threats?"

"I don't know what you're talking about," Thornton said. His tone of voice sounded truthful. "Who received death threats?"

"The whole Beaumont family," I said. "Tell me this, Counselor, did anyone from Ashtree Farms visit your office in the last hour or so?"

"What kind of a question is that?"

"Just answer it, okay?"

He shook his head. "No, I don't think I will."

"The other day," I said, "you received a visit from Shirley Beaumont. Mind telling me the purpose of the visit?"

A frown scooted briefly across Thornton's face. There was disbelief in his voice. "Mr. Rhineheart, are you having my office watched?"

I nodded. "You can't make a move without me knowing about it, Counselor."

"You may not know it, Mr. Rhineheart, but by that

admission you just put yourself in an actionable position. If you don't leave," he said, "I will call the police and have them arrest you for criminal trespass."

I sat still a moment and then I stood up. It was time to leave. I was trying to come up with a good exit line, but I couldn't think of anything. What would John Wayne have said in a situation like this? I walked to the door, then I turned and looked at Thornton, who was glaring at me. He pointed an admonishing finger in my direction and said, "You needn't worry, Mr. Rhineheart, your unprofessional behavior here will not go unreported. I can assure you of that. Expect some trouble on your next attempt to renew your investigator's license."

I smiled, pleased that Thornton had stayed true to character and in the best straight-man tradition had provided me with something to respond to. The problem was that I could not bring myself to utter the obvious response that *trouble was my business*. Instead, in my politest voice I said, "Good afternoon, Counselor. Have a nice day."

TWENTY-SEVEN

AFTER I left Thornton's office I drove over to the Oxford Manor Nursing Home. It was doubtful that the identity of the man Betty Walker had visited was important, but it was one of the little tag-end things that needed to be checked out. I parked in the nursing home lot and before I got out of the car, I took out my wallet and flipped through the various business cards I'd accumulated. I came across one that read:

MELVIN GOODROW
Investigator
State Bureau of Statistical Services

I stuck it in my pocket and entered the building by a side door. There were stairs and tile floors and off-white walls and a long corridor lined with offices on both sides. A neatly lettered RECORDS OFFICE hung above an open door halfway down the corridor.

Inside the door was a room with a desk and a long counter. The walls were lined with filing cabinets. A plump black-haired girl wearing a snug white uniform with a plastic name tag that read DAWN was standing at the counter, flipping the pages of a *People* magazine.

She looked at me and smiled. Dimples appeared in her cheeks. "How can I help you?"

I looked at her body and bit back the reply that occurred to me. I handed her my card and said, "I'm with the state Statistical Resources Department and I'm here to do a survey on visitation procedures. Let's see," I said, taking a slip of paper out of my pocket and pretending to consult it, "your institution deals with the mentally handicapped. Is that right?"

Dawn nodded. "Except we call them 'special needs patients' now. We deal with children and adults."

"And I assume you keep a record of visits to your residents. What we're interested in is a sample grouping. Which patients were visited, for example, today. By whom? That sort of thing..."

She frowned down at the card I'd handed her. "I never heard of the State Bureau of Statistics."

"We're a new agency," I said. "We get our funding from a combination of sources, public and private."

She smiled. "Sure you do, and my name's Dolly Parton."

"Actually," I said, "you look a little like Dolly."

"Dolly got blond hair. Mine's black."

"And beautiful," I said, "but I wasn't really talking about your hair."

She smiled again. "Flattery'll get you almost anywhere you want to."

"Will it get me a little information?"

"You mean like a phone number?"

"Well, I was thinking more along the lines of the name of the gentleman that Mrs. Walker visited today."

"She have sandy-colored hair?"

I nodded. "The man was in a wheelchair. She pushed him around the grounds."

"How come you want to know who he is? What are you anyway? A private eye, or somethin'?"

"How'd you guess?"

Dawn let out a squeal. "For real? You're a private eye?" She eyed me up and down. "Lord, I never met any private eyes before. I wasn't sure they really existed ...except in movies or on the tube."

"We're in real life, too," I assured her. "A few of us anyway."

"I'm not supposed to give out any information about patients without authorization."

"All I need is a name."

"I could get in deep trouble."

"Only if somebody found out. And I'd never tell."

"I don't even know who you are." She looked at the card. "Your name's not Melvin. You don't look like a Melvin."

"It's Rhineheart."

"*Who?*"

"Rhineheart. Michael."

"What kind of a name is that?"

"Michael?"

"The other."

I shrugged. "My father was German. My mother was Irish."

She propped her chin on her hand and leaned toward me. "You know who you remind me of?"

"Your brother?"

"No, silly." She waited for me to ask.

"Who?"

"You remind me of that actor who used to play a private eye in the movies. You look like he used to look when he was young. I don't know if he's dead now or what."

"I remind you of a dead guy?"

"I don't think he's dead. I just don't see him anymore. He's old now."

"I remind you of an old guy?"

"What *was* his name?"

"I don't know," I said.

"He had this really masterful chin."

"Cary Grant?" I said with no real hope.

She smirked. "Don't be silly. This guy had a crooked nose like you." She wrote something down on a piece of paper, folded it up, and handed it to me. "Don't open it up until you get outside."

"What about the patient Ms. Walker was visiting?"

Dawn looked over her shoulder to see if anyone was listening, "Her brother," she said.

"Her brother?"

Dawn nodded. "She comes to see him every week."

A stern-faced woman in a starched white coat appeared in the doorway. She glared at us. "Dawn," she said in a piercing voice, "I want Mr. Proctor's chart."

"Yes, Mrs. Fisher." Before she turned away, Dawn threw me a little wave.

Outside, as I was walking to my car, I opened the slip of paper. It contained the name *Robert Mitchum*, and underneath that it said, *Dawn Adams, 656–7658.*

TWENTY-EIGHT

I drove downtown to the office, which was empty and full of musty air. I threw open a window and sat down behind my desk. I leaned back in the swivel chair and put my feet up on the desk and considered the situation. It was 1:30 on Friday afternoon. The Queen's plane was due in Sunday afternoon, which gave me fifty-some hours to solve the case. Having a deadline was a new experience. Something like having a sword hanging over your head. If Betty Walker had returned to the trailer park, she was probably home by now. I put my feet down, picked up the phone, and dialed John Reardon at Midtown Investigations. Besides being a first-rate private investigator, John was an old friend, who owed me a couple of favors.

"What's going on, Rhine?" Reardon asked.

"I'm calling in markers, John."

"What do you need?" Reardon said.

"I need a full-time surveillance team," I said, "to watch and follow somebody named Betty Walker."

"What's she look like and where does she live?"

I told him. I described the Chevette.

Reardon said he would put his best three people on it and get back to me periodically.

"Fair enough," I said. "This'll make us even, John."

"Whatever."

After I hung up, I took out the folders of material McGraw had researched. Maybe there was something in there I had missed. I was going through an article about Ashtree's management practices when the phone rang.

I picked it up. LT said, "I got that information you wanted on Walker. He did three to five at Eddyville for hanging paper. Released on good behavior in 1979."

"Good work, LT. Anything on the pickup?"

"I'm working on it, Rhine. I'll call you the minute I get something."

I thanked LT and hung up the phone. I went back to the article. Two minutes later, the phone rang again.

Katz's raspy voice came over the wire. "Peep."

"What can I do for you, Sergeant?"

"Meet me at Shirley Beaumont's place in ten minutes. Her address is—"

"I know where she lives," I said with a sinking feeling in my stomach.

"*Used to*," Katz said. "*Used to live* is the right way to put that, Peeper."

A half dozen squad cars, their blue lights flashing, stood in the street in front of Shirley Beaumont's mansion. Along the block, groups of neighbors stood in front of their homes, peering at the Beaumont place.

A uniformed cop was guarding the front door. I told him who I was and he nodded and said, "Uh-huh, Katz is waiting for you in the front room."

The front room was a spacious parlor with a tall ceiling, a crystal chandelier, gold sconces on the wall. It was filled with overstuffed furniture. The windows were lined with plush gold drapes closed against the afternoon sun. Katz was standing in the center of the room, talking to an overweight guy in a rumpled suit. The guy had thinning hair, wore glasses, and carried a small black bag. Katz didn't look too happy to see me, but he crooked a finger for me to come over.

"Rhineheart, meet Doc Parker. He's filling in for the assistant city medical examiner, who's on vacation."

THE QUEEN'S MARE

We shook hands. Katz said, "Rhineheart here's a hotshit private eye who knew the dead individuals."

Parker nodded, a bored look on his face. He said, "The victims have been dead for close to twelve hours, maybe longer. I put time of death somewhere between one and three A.M."

"That the best you can do, Doc?"

"It's the best anyone can do." He turned and shuffled out of the room.

"Want to see the corpses, Peep?"

"Not especially."

But Katz had already turned and was leaving the room. I caught up to him in the hallway. He stopped in front of a door on the left and opened it. We entered. The room was a bedroom, occupied by a couple of uniforms, two technicians taking fiber and fingerprint samples, and a photographer who stood next to a king-sized bed, taking pictures of the couple stretched across it. Shirley Beaumont and her trainer Terri.

The bed was soaked with their blood. They were dressed in nightgowns, their bodies lying at angles to each other. They both had been shot. Terri with a single bullet in the temple. Shirley Beaumont, on the other hand, had been shot a number of times squarely in the center part of her face, which no longer resembled a face.

I had seen worse sights, but not too many. I thought about Hattie Beaumont.

"Mrs. Beaumont know about it yet?"

"Captain's calling her right now." Katz pointed at Shirley. "She might have been a dyke, but I hear she was a good-looking broad. She don't look too pretty now, does she?"

Someone in the room snickered.

"What caliber weapon?"

"A .22," Katz said. "A woman's gun."

I thought back to my conversation with Diane Carter.

"And look what I found." Katz snapped a business

card between his fingers like a playing card. "Guess whose card this is, Peeper?"

"I don't have to guess, Katz. I know whose card it is."

"I found it on a bench in the gym room."

"So what?"

"Card means you were here. Recently. I want to know when and I want to know why."

"I'm not sure I'm going to tell you all that. Some of it's confidential information. Privileged."

"Privileged my ass. There ain't no such a goddamn thing with dead people. You fucking better tell me what I want to know, or I'll take you downtown, book you for obstruction of justice, witholding information on a capital case. That's a fucking felony, Peeper."

"You keep threatening me, Sergeant, I'm going to piss my pants in a minute."

One of the technicians chuckled. Katz gave him a look and he coughed and cleared his throat. Katz stuck a finger in my face. "Peeper, I don't need to threaten you. I got a neighbor-type eyewitness seen you out here yesterday afternoon. You know what that makes you? A fucking suspect, that's what. You were here. You deny being here?"

"No," I said. "I was here."

"How come?"

"Shirley Beaumont wanted to see me."

"What about?"

"She wanted to hire me as a bodyguard."

"A bodyguard?"

"She told me she'd received some death threats, and she was frightened."

Katz looked as if he didn't believe a word of it. "In the first place," he said, "why would she hire *you*, Peep. You're the dude who got zonkered on the head and lost her mama's money. In the second place, what is this 'death threats' dreck? That's the first time I heard about any death threats connected to this case. And who the fuck gets death threats anyway? That's out of a book somewhere."

"All the Beaumonts have received death threats recently," I said. "Check it out."

"Don't worry. I'll check it out. I don't need no gumshoe to tell me to check things out." A vein in Katz's neck began to pulse.

"Actually, now that you know it, it wouldn't hurt if you assigned somebody to watch the family for a while."

"You think it wouldn't hurt, huh? You think the police force got nothing better to do than watch over some rich broads who been getting telephone threats, Peeper? Well, we appreciate the advice, but in the meantime we got a double homicide here to solve, and the fact is, you been witholding information about this case right from the beginning. You don't start being cooperative I'm going to take you downtown and sit on you. What have you got to say to that?"

"Kiss my ass, motherfucker." It was out of my mouth before I could stop it.

Katz smiled and gestured to one of the uniforms. "Barnes, I want you to read Rhineheart here his rights, search him, cuff him, then take him downtown, and book him for obstructing justice and withholding information."

Barnes got a nervous look on his face, I smiled at him and said, "Don't worry, Barnes, I'll go quietly." I took my Python out of my shoulder holster and handed it to Katz, butt first. "Be careful with that, Sergeant. It's loaded. I've got a license for it and I want it back when I'm released."

Then I turned around, put my hands on the wall, and assumed the position.

TWENTY-NINE

DOWNTOWN, they booked me and let me make one phone call. I phoned McGraw, who had just gotten out of bed and was barely coherent.

"Who is this?"

"What do you mean 'Who is this?' It's Rhineheart. Don't you recognize my voice?"

"What time is it?" she asked.

I told her it was 4:30.

"In the *afternoon*?"

"Yeah, in the afternoon."

"What am I doing getting up at this time of day?"

"I just called you. You were up all night on the stakeout. Remember?"

"Oh, yeah. Where are you?"

"I'm in jail. You're my one phone call. I need you to call my lawyer."

"What are you in jail for?"

"Shirley Beaumont was murdered this afternoon."

"Oh God."

"They booked me for withholding information. Call my lawyer."

McGraw said she'd get right on it, then she paused and wanted to know what to do if Flynn wasn't available. You know how he is, she said, when the track's open he's never around.

I told her to get me somebody. She said not to worry, she'd have me sprung in a few hours.

172

They kept me in a holding cell with two winos until 6:30 P.M. when they brought me upstairs to Katz's office. Katz sat behind his desk. Dixon, the state cop, was there. So was Washburn, the states attorney guy. There was a local assistant prosecutor, a short, stocky man in shirt sleeves and tie who was holding a sheaf of official-looking papers.

An attractive black-haired woman wearing a tailored business suit was sitting in a chair in front of Katz's desk. She stood up and smiled when I entered. "I'm Ellen Wade," she said, and when she spoke she made it clear she was speaking directly to me, "I'm your attorney."

She gave me her hand. "It's a pleasure to meet you, Mr. Rhineheart. Sally's told me a lot about you."

Old McGraw. "Call me 'Michael.'"

"My advice is to answer no questions and if we go before a judge to let me speak for you." I looked over and saw that everyone else in the room was glaring at her. I smiled and said, "Whatever you say, Counselor."

"Who said anything about court, Ellen?" the stocky man said. "We simply wanted to talk to Mr. Rhineheart about his involvement with the Beaumont family. If he cooperates, we're prepared to drop all charges and release him in your custody."

Ms. Wade shook her head. "Not good enough, Sam. The charges are pure fiction. They won't stand a judge's quick glance. They're not only fiction, they're malicious. My advice to Mr. Rhineheart is going to be on the order of bringing a false arrest suit against the city, perhaps even going to Federal Court to petition for an injunction against the police department for deliberately violating his civil rights."

"Oh, for Christ sakes, Ellen."

"I'm dead serious, Sam."

"Well, maybe we can work something out," the stocky man said. "What, uh, would ameliorate things?"

"Drop all charges, release my client immediately, and

we'll give serious consideration to not filing a false arrest suit."

"No consideration. We'll drop the charges and release him in return for your assurance there will be no action taken against the city."

Ellen Wade nodded. "Done." She looked at me and winked.

I picked up my wallet and my shoulder holster and weapon from the property room downstairs. McGraw was waiting in the hallway. She and Ellen Wade exchanged a greeting and a hug. McGraw said, "There's *beaucoup* reporters in the lobby. They want to talk to you about the murder."

"We better cut out the back way," I said.

I thanked Ms. Wade and told her to send me a bill. She smiled, said she owed McGraw a favor, and gave me her hand. "Good luck and stay out of trouble," she said.

"You married?" I asked her.

She shook her head.

"You go with anybody?"

She nodded. I let go of her hand. "Too bad," I said.

"Bye." She turned and left the room. I glanced over at McGraw, who was giving me a bad look.

"You got to hit on everything that walks?" she said. "Including my friends?"

"I wasn't hitting on her," I said. "I just asked her if she was available, that's all."

"You were hitting on her," McGraw said, "but that's all right, you can't help yourself. It's one of your major character defects."

The rear basement exit of the police station let us out in an alley behind Jefferson Street. There were no reporters around, and none followed us to the parking lot. McGraw drove me over to pick up my car, and on the way I filled her in on the rest of the day's events.

The only thing that seemed to interest her was Betty Walker. "You just *let her go back to the trailer*?" she said.

"Not exactly," I said, "but it wasn't that big a deal. I had other things to do that were more important."

"If it wasn't that big a deal, then why did I spend all night out there on a stakeout?"

"It was necessary. You did a good job. It's just that I wanted to go see Thornton and check out the old guy. When I got back to the office I arranged for Reardon to pick up the stakeout."

"You lost her, didn't you?"

"What are you talking about?"

"Did you lose her, or not?"

"Sort of."

"This is one I may not let you forget. Ever."

"I was never that good at shadowing somebody. As a dick, it's not one of my strong points. Ask Farns."

"Don't worry," she said. "I will."

It was a little past seven when she dropped me off. I told her I was going to meet Farnsworth at O'Brien's at nine and that I'd see her then. Inside my apartment I picked up the phone and dialed Ashtree Farms. Paige answered the phone.

"I'm sorry about what happened to your aunt," I said. "How is Mrs. Beaumont?"

"She's in her room. I don't think she's doing very well."

"Let me talk to Diane Carter," I said.

When she came on the line Diane Carter said, "Thank you for calling, Michael."

"How is she?"

"She collapsed when she heard the news. She's in her bed. The doctor's on his way."

"If there's anything I can do, let me know."

"Thank you, Michael. I will."

I got cleaned up and drove over to Mama Grisanti's

restaurant in Dupont Square and ordered dinner: cannelloni, bread and cheese, and wine. I barely touched the food, but I drank three glasses of wine and thought about the case. When I left I drove over to O'Brien's.

THIRTY

I arrived there a few minutes before nine. McGraw and Farnsworth were seated in the back booth, arguing about pool.

"I give you the damn game," Farnsworth said.

"Give hell," McGraw said, "I won it fair and square. You missed the easiest gimme on the nine ball I ever seen."

"My eye went bad on me there. Fogged over. Blurred up."

"You choked."

"Choked my ass. I been playing nine ball since before you was born, girlie."

I slid in across from them and gestured for Wanda Jean, the night waitress, who was working the booths and the tables. Wanda Jean was wearing a tight sweater and tighter jeans. She wore long false lashes and lots of bright red lipstick. Her current hair shade was blond. It looked good on her. Wanda Jean and I were, as she put it, "particular" friends.

"Give these two whatever they're drinking and give me a tall Maker's and water."

"I don't see you around as often as I used to," Wanda Jean said.

"I don't get around as often as I want to," I said.

"That could be the first two lines of a country-and-western song," McGraw said brightly. Wanda Jean looked at her as if she was crazy. "Two beers and a

Maker's Mark and water," she said and headed toward the bar.

"I heard about your day, kid," Farnsworth said. "Can't say I was surprised to see the first victim turn out to be Shirley Beaumont. It sorta figured."

"What do you mean *first*?" McGraw asked. "Are there going to be more killings?"

Farns nodded. "Prolly. Almost always is."

"Let's hope not," I said.

Wanda Jean brought the drinks to the booth, leaned over and whispered, "I get off early tonight," in my ear, smiled at Farnsworth, gave McGraw a bad look, grabbed up the empties, and departed.

"What's new on your end?" I asked Farnsworth.

"Old Graves is a busy fellow. He's got crack houses in four different locations and girls all over the city. He spends a lot of time in his nightclub, the one Shirley Beaumont owned part of. I was busy follering him all day. He didn't go anywhere near Shirley Beaumont's house." Farnsworth swallowed half his beer. "But you know something, kid," he said, "these stakeouts aren't paying off. They're not leading us to Eddie Walker, and he's the key. We got to find him. How about I go over to that farm in Lexington where he used to work? Talk to the people he used to work with. See if I can find someone who knows Eddie and his habits."

"Sounds like a good idea to me, old man."

Farnsworth turned to McGraw. "How'd you like to go along, girlie?"

McGraw said, "You're asking *me* to go with you?"

Farnsworth nodded.

McGraw turned to me. "What about it?"

I shook my head. "I need you for something else. Eddie Walker grew up in an orphanage around here. I want you to check out all the orphanages in Louisville and Jefferson County and the surrounding counties. We need files on people who knew him. Anything like that."

McGraw smiled. "That's even better," she said. "My very own assignment. It's about time you gave me something responsible to do."

Farnsworth looked suddenly glum and said, "When I was a young man, no dames wanted to be a private eye. They wanted to be housewives or somebody's girlfriend and ones that didn't want to be housewives and girlfriends wanted to be secretaries and bookkeepers and stuff like that."

McGraw poked Farnsworth in the ribs. "When *you* were a young man, people still lived in caves, you old shit." She looked over my left shoulder and frowned. "Uh-oh. What do we have here?"

I turned around in time to see Lucky Thompson and his bodyguard approaching the booth. Farnsworth let out a whistle when he saw Ruben's size. Ruben was wearing the same beachcomber's outfit he'd worn the other day, but he looked bigger, as if he had somehow grown some since our last encounter. Then I realized that it was the first time I had seen him on his feet. He was as big as a building.

Farnsworth said, "What can we do for y'all?"

Thompson said, "Ah'm Lucky Thompson. This here"—he jerked a thumb at his companion—"is Ruben. He's ma bodyguard."

Farnsworth nodded at Ruben. "Hello, Ruben."

Ruben didn't react. He didn't look at Farnsworth. He just stared into space with a flat, blank look on his face.

"Ruben don't socialize," Thompson said. "He's ma bodyguard. That's all he does."

"Twenty-four hours a *day*?" McGraw asked.

"Seven days a week," Thompson said.

"Does he sleep outside your door?" Farnsworth said.

Thompson nodded. "As a matter of fact, he does."

"Does he follow you into the toilet?" Farnsworth wanted to know.

"That ain't any of your bidness," Thompson said.

"What do you need a bodyguard for anyway?" Farnsworth asked.

"I been over that already with your friend here." He pointed at me, then addressed me: "I tol' you I'd be back to see you."

"Answer's still the same," I said. "No."

"I'm looking for something different this time. I want to buy that there card you found in Walker's place."

"It's not for sale."

"Me and Ruben don't take 'it's not for sale' for an answer," Lucky said. "What we figure is there's some kind of price you'd be willing to accept. Your continued good health, for example."

"I'm kind of slow," I said, "but that sounds like a threat."

"Call it whatever you like."

Farnsworth shook his head. "Bad mistake to threaten the kid," he said.

"You keep out of it, old fart," Thompson said to Farnsworth.

I stood up. "The old fart speaks for me," I said.

When I stood up Ruben made a sound from deep within his chest and moved in behind his boss. Things, it appeared, were escalating fairly quickly.

I told Thompson, "Have that goon of yours back off, or there'll be some shit to pay."

"Me and Ruben don't back off," Thompson said. "If you get into a confrontation with us, it's you-all who's gonna do the backing off."

"Why don't you take off to the Ladies Room," I said to McGraw.

"Bullshit," McGraw said, getting to her feet, "if there's going to be some trouble, I want to get my share of it."

Lucky Thompson looked at McGraw. "It don't make no difference to Ruben what he hits. Man or a lady."

"That's good," McGraw said, "'cause I ain't no fucking lady, Jack."

"My name ain't Jack," Thomspon said angrily.

"Your name is shit as far as I'm concerned," McGraw said.

Farnsworth stood up. He pointed a finger at Ruben. "The bigger they come, the harder they fall, pal."

A number of things happened quickly then.

Ruben reached over and lifted Farnsworth off his feet and flung him across the room.

McGraw let out a bloodcurdling karate shriek and jabbed her fingers into Lucky Thompson's face.

Thompson dropped to the ground and scuttled under the table.

McGraw reached behind me, picked up Farn's beer bottle and smashed it upside Ruben's head. Ruben barely flinched. What he did was make another sound in his chest and stretch his arms out in an attempt to wrap me up in a bear hug.

I cut loose with a left hook–right cross combination to Ruben's face and danced sideways out of his reach. The punches had no effect on the big man except to make slight red spots appear where they landed. Ruben turned toward me and raised his fists, which were the size of small bowling balls. At that point McGraw leaped up on his back. When Ruben reached back to fling her off I stepped forward and kicked him squarely in the balls. I put some effort into it, as if I were trying out for the punter position on an N.F.L. squad. A loud groan burst forth from Ruben's lips. He forgot about McGraw and instead reached down to tend to his groin area.

McGraw hopped off Ruben's back and I whipped out the Python, reversed it, brought it down just hard enough and in the right place on Ruben's head to take him out. His huge body collapsed in stages, like a building being demolished. It swayed and tottered, then folded up on itself. It pitched forward, falling slowly and heavily to the floor, rattling all the bottles behind the bar.

The customers at O'Brien's broke into applause.

THIRTY-ONE

I went down the line of booths to look for Farnsworth and found McGraw helping him to his feet. He had no broken bones or visible bruises and seemed to be all right, but his face was as white as a sheet of McGraw's typing paper.

He took out his upper plate, inspected it, then stuck it back in his mouth and said, "They didn't know who they was fucking with, did they, kid?"

"That's one way of putting it," I said. I looked at McGraw. "You could've got hurt jumping up on that monster's back."

"Are you chewing me out, or what? I thought I made a couple of pretty good moves"—she hesitated—"for a broad."

"You did all right," I said.

"So what happened?" Farnsworth asked. "Did we win or lose?"

"I'd say we won this one." I asked McGraw, "What do you think?"

McGraw nodded. "Definitely. Put it down in the win column." We looked toward the rear where Thompson was standing over Ruben trying to wake him. "Make it a T.K.O. in the second."

Farnsworth put his hat on and smoothed out the brim. "I believe I'm going home and hit the sack then. One fight a night is about all I can handle anymore."

"Good idea," I said.

"'Night, kid." Farnsworth made a little gun out of his finger and thumb and pointed it at McGraw. "I'll see you tomorrow, girlie." He headed across the room toward the door.

I turned to McGraw and said, "Why don't you follow him and make sure he gets home okay?"

"Beneath that shoulder-holstered exterior, you're just a big softhearted lug, aren't you?"

"If that was true," I said, "I'd be following him myself. Not asking you."

"That's a good point," McGraw said. "Hey, Farns," she yelled. "Wait up." She hurried out the door.

I felt a touch at my elbow. I spun around to find Wanda Jean smiling at me. She pointed to the phone on the wall next to the jukebox. "You got a telephone call."

It was the answering service, a woman with a brisk businesslike voice. "Mr. Rhineheart, you keep getting a message from someone who says it's an emergency and who wants you to return his call immediately. He called three times in the last ten minutes and said to tell you that it's Eddie W. and that you would know what he meant." She gave me the number and I jammed a quarter in the phone and dialed it immediately.

It rang once, was picked up, and Eddie Walker's voice said, "Is this the private cop?"

"What do you want, Eddie?" Out of the corner of my eye, I saw Thompson helping his bodyguard out the door.

"You got to help me. I'm in some deep shit, man. I thought I knew these people, but I don't. They're loonies. A crazy family. I didn't have any idea of what they really wanted. These fucking people are talking murder. And they're capable of it. Believe me. I want to make some kind of a deal, Rhineheart. You got any friends on the police? I want you to put me in touch with someone who can make a deal."

"Where are you?"

"Where am I? I'm in a fucking phone booth on the corner of Fifth and Jefferson, but I got to get back. These fuckers *check* on me . . . man. I can't talk now. I'll call you back."

"Wait—"

But Walker had hung up.

I took a seat at the bar and ordered a drink. I stared at my reflection in the mirror above a row of bottles. The reason Walker had called was apparent. You could hear the fear in his voice. But who was he afraid of? What bunch of loonies? What family? Was he talking about the Beaumonts? If not, who else? Walker had mentioned the possibility of murder, as if he didn't know that one had taken place. Maybe he didn't. Shirley Beaumont's homicide had not been discovered until late in the afternoon and maybe it had not become public knowledge yet.

Walker's call was one more item to add to the shapeless pile of information that was accumulating in my head. Fifth and Jefferson. Fifth and Jefferson. What was at Fifth and Jefferson? The courthouse. The county clerk's headquarters. Thornton's office. Professional office buildings. Fifth and Jefferson was around the corner from a half dozen hotels. Maybe Walker was staying in one. He said he had to get back. Back to where?

I ordered another drink, looked at my watch. It was ten o'clock. I went over to the phone and dialed the Seelbach. The same snooty clerk answered the phone and connected me to Charlotte's room.

Wallace Thornton answered the phone.

"This is Michael Rhineheart," I said. "I'm calling to see if Charlotte's all right."

"Just a minute," Thornton said.

After a moment, Charlotte came on the line. "Michael," she said, "how gracious of you to call."

"I'm sorry about Shirley," I said. "Are you all right?"

"As well as could be expected, I suppose."

"Do you need anything?"

"Thank you for offering, but no." Her voice threatened to tremble.

"How is your grandmother?"

"She's bearing up," Charlotte said. She turned away from the phone a moment and I heard her ask Thornton to be a dear and pour her another drink.

"I'll let you go," I said. "Again, I'm sorry about your sister."

"Thank you, Michael. I'll talk to you soon." She hung up, and I went back to the bar and sat down. Sam brought me a drink. Wanda Jean came up and stood behind me. I addressed her reflection across the bar. "What time did you say you got off?"

"I didn't," Wanda Jean said, "but for your information it's midnight."

I nodded. "I'll wait."

The piercing jangle of the telephone woke me. I raised up and looked at the digital face of the clock beside the bed: 4:34. I picked up the receiver. A muffled but recognizable voice said, "You don't get off the case, you're the next dead one," and hung up.

Next to me, Wanda Jean stirred. "Who's calling this hour?" she muttered.

"It was just a death threat," I said. "Go back to sleep." I pressed the button that transferred all calls to the answering machine.

"Okay." She lay still for a moment, then sat up abruptly. "A death threat? Honest to God?"

"Somebody wants me off this case, Wanda Jean."

"I guess they do," she said. "What did they say?"

I repeated the voice's message.

"Are you going to do what they want?"

"I doubt it."

"I didn't think you would," Wanda Jean said. "You hardly ever do what other people want you to do, do you?"

"I try not to."

"You sure do lead a strange wild kind of life. Death threats and gettin' shot at 'n fightin' and carryin' on. Why is that, do you suppose?"

I shrugged. "It's just the way things go down when you do what I do."

"Don't you ever get scared, Rhineheart?"

"I *stay* scared, babe."

"You don't act like it."

"That's a big front. Just tonight my secretary was saying that deep down inside I'm softhearted and sensitive."

"You mean that little person with the frizzy hair?"

"Her name's McGraw."

"How tall is she anyway?"

"She claims to be five feet, but I don't know..."

"More like four ten."

"She's small, but she's good people."

"I won't say nothing bad about her," Wanda Jean said. "I'm a softhearted sensitive person my own self."

"You're damn right you are," I said.

"But I'm chicken. When I hear about death threats, I get chills up and down my spine. I need somebody to hold me."

I reached over and put my arms around her. "That better?"

"It sure is."

"I tell you what," I said. "Why don't you put your arms around me, too? I could use a little hugging myself."

Wanda Jean put her arms around me.

"You know what else?" I said.

"Huh?"

"This hugging and holding is a fine thing, but I got a feeling that it's going to lead to something else."

Wanda Jean giggled. "I'm getting that very feeling myself," she said.

THIRTY-TWO

In the morning when I opened my eyes Wanda Jean was coming out of the bathroom. She was dressed and her hair was still wet from the shower. Wanda Jean was in her late thirties and without her makeup you could see the little lines around her eyes. I liked the lines. They added something—character, or something—to her face. Wanda Jean grabbed her purse off the table.

"Don't even ask me where I'm going," she said. "I got six million things to do, sugar. A doctor's appointment and I got to go by the store and a whole bunch of stuff." She leaned down and kissed me. "I'll catch you the next time," she said. "Call me."

After she left, I got up and put on some running clothes. Before I left I punched the replay button on the telephone. Between 7:15 and 8:20 there had been six calls, all from the newspaper and local television stations. They wanted a comment on Shirley Beaumont's murder.

I drove over to Bellarmine, parked, and ran three miles. To cool down, I walked another mile, and was on the last lap when the stretch limo with the dark windows pulled up and parked on the shoulder of the road. I went over to the car.

Today, Graves was wearing a shadow-stripe brown silk suit, the same Ray Ban shades, and a somber, worried look.

"You're awful dressed up for Saturday morning," I said.

Wordlessly, Graves handed me the morning edition of the newspaper. The headline read, *Prominent Socialite Murdered. Beaumont Heir Found Dead in Old Louisville Mansion.*

"Bitch owed me twenty large, R."

"Don't tell nobody that, Graves. They'll probably think twenty thousand is a good motive for offing somebody."

"But you and I know better than that, R. We know if someone owes you big money, you're gonna bust your ass keeping them alive."

"I guess," I said, my eye caught by a sidebar adjoining the murder story: *Thoroughbred Horse Reported Stolen.* I flipped back to the sports section and checked yesterday's results. The last race exacta had come three two eight. The two horse had gotten between my horses.

"R., you gonna read the paper, or talk to me?"

"What'd you want to see me about, Graves?"

"I'm going down to the Islands for a few weeks... until this thing chills out. If the police talk to you about my ex-partner, I want you to tell them the straight shit, R. Tell them how concerned I was about her welfare. If you like, tell them about our little talks. How I offered you help. How I was always looking after her interests."

"Sure," I said. "I'll tell them, but they might think you came and talked to me in order to set up an alibi."

"Hey, I can't help what they thinkin'. Just tell them the truth, okay?"

"Sure. And what do you want me to tell the reporters?"

"*Reporters?* 'Fuck you talking about?"

"I didn't tell you about them calling me up?"

"Who? The reporters?"

"Yeah."

"Oh shit," Graves said. "Don't tell me no reporters are on to this end of it. That's all I need. They like dogs after a scent. They like you, R., they don't quit. They get on a thing, they never give up. Reporters ask you about me, don't say anything, man."

"I'll tell them no comment," I said.

"Don't tell them nothing. Pretend you don't know me." Graves spoke to his driver: "Start it up, Thurel. Let's get the fuck out of here."

The automatic door opened and I stepped out. "Have a nice trip, Curtis." I slammed the car door. The limo roared off, spinning gravel against my leg. Something told me that I wouldn't be seeing Curtis Graves for a while.

I drove home slowly, took a shower, and got dressed. I didn't bother to shave. I told myself the Queen wasn't coming until Sunday anyway. It wasn't much of a joke. My standard office outfit was sport coat and slacks. A button-down dress shirt. No tie. A pair of soft leather loafers. I drove downtown.

A white van with a satellite dish mounted on its roof was parked in front of the building. Big black letters on the side of the van advertised *Channel 9 Louisville's Only Instavideo Cam*.

I parked the Maverick behind the van and got out. Almost immediately, two men, a cameraman with a portable video camera on his shoulder and a reporter waving a microphone, emerged from the van and headed my way. The cameraman was a small black guy wearing a U of L sweatshirt. He stopped near the doorway and began to record the scene while the reporter, who was tall and thin and wore a beard, continued toward me.

"Mr. Rhinehurt, may we have a word with you?" The reporter's polite tone of voice was belied by the look on his face, which reminded me of the look of a hungry dog when it spotted some food.

He planted himself on the sidewalk in front of me.

"Mr. Rhinehat, is it true that you were hired to find a broodmare that was stolen from Ashtree Farms?"

"My name is Rhineheart."

"Would you care to comment on Shirley Beaumont's murder and whether or not it is related to the missing broodmare?"

"No, I wouldn't." I started to make a flanking move around the reporter, and as I did, I noticed in the corner of my eye a red pickup truck come to a halt in the street alongside the TV van. The truck window was open and I could see the driver in profile. He had a thin face and was wearing glasses and a trucker's cap. As I watched, the driver reached behind him with both hands and took what looked like a double-barreled shotgun off a gun rack, twisted around, and swung both barrels of the weapon out the window.

It took me a second to realize that a guy in a red pickup was pointing a gun at me. I started to hold up a hand and say, "Hey, wait a minute," but then I thought, *What the fuck am I doing?*, and hit the ground, dropping quickly to the sidewalk and in the process shouldering aside the reporter who also went sprawling to the ground, scattering his microphone and notebook along the curb.

The shotgun went off and the air all around me reverberated with the boom of the shotgun blast, which was followed immediately by the ripping, cracking sound of large sheets of glass breaking. With my face pressed to the cement, I felt a shower of glass fragments raining down on me. The glass downpour seemed to last forever. But when it was over I pushed myself up off the ground and as I reached for my weapon, I heard the truck roar off, tires squealing.

On my feet, I aimed the Python at the retreating truck and squeezed off a pair of shots, one of which whanged off the cab roof. Holding the gun out in front of me with two hands, I stood there, sucking in large amounts of air and exhaling noisily. My heart was banging against my chest, but at the same time I felt abruptly tired, as if I had just gone fifteen rounds with someone who was way too big and much too bad for me.

I lowered the gun slowly, conscious that I was being watched. I turned around to find that the large plate glass windows of The Bistro had disappeared. Inside, a dozen customers sat at linen-covered tables, looking stunned, peering out at the street. An upscale-type head waiter in white shirt and black tie stood near where the window used to be. He had a dumbfounded look on his face. I couldn't resist it. I said to him, "That's what you get for putting your pissant little joint below my office," but the waiter didn't appear to hear me and made no reply. He was staring at the Python hanging down at my side.

I looked over to my left and saw that the cameraman had not moved from his spot on the sidewalk and was continuing to record the scene. Apparently, he had caught the event on videotape. "You get the shooter?" I asked.

The cameraman looked up from his viewfinder and shook his head. "Just you," he said, "and old Terry there." He pointed at the reporter, who was lying face-down on the sidewalk with his hands covering his head. "Hey, Terry," he called. "It's all right. All the shit is over now." Terry raised his head and looked around, but made no move to get up. "Hey, man, it's all right," the cameraman said. "You won't believe some of the footage I got. I can't wait to see what it looks like."

I put my weapon in its holster and stepped around the cameraman.

"Hey," the black guy said, "ole Terry there gonna have a whole lot of questions to ask you."

"I'm not taking any more questions today," I said and entered the building. I took the stairs two at a time and when I reached the top I saw that the outer door to my office was standing open. With McGraw out hunting down orphanages and Farns over in Lexington, the door should have been closed and locked. I felt my pulse start to race, a tingle of anxiety in the tips of my fingers.

I took out the Python and held it at my side. I stepped into the room, raised the weapon, and said, "Freeze," to a darkly clad figure near the windows.

THIRTY-THREE

THE figure turned.

It was Charlotte Beaumont, swathed in black: dress, stockings, shoes, gloves, and a chic black hat with a veil. The large brimmed hat made her look like the mystery woman in an old Warner Brothers melodrama about international intrigue. The mourning outfit did nothing to disguise her lissome figure. If anything, in fact, the straight sober lines of the dress enhanced it.

Charlotte spoke through the veil. "Why are you pointing a gun at me, Michael? Are you going to shoot me?"

I lowered the weapon.

"I thought after the other night, the last thing in the world you'd want to do to me is shoot me."

"I'm sorry," I said, putting the weapon in my holster. "I got carried away."

"Was there some sort of commotion downstairs?" Charlotte inquired.

"Nothing important," I said. "How'd you get in here, anyway?"

"I had the building super let me in," Charlotte said. "So I'd have a place to sit while I waited for you. He was very kind."

I bet he was, I thought. Who the hell wouldn't be kind to Charlotte? Once they got a good look at her?

Charlotte sighed, a sound that was sorrowful and theatrical at the same time. "I understand," she said in a voice that trembled, "that you saw my dear sister shortly after she was slain. Saw her in her blood, in the very bed she was murdered in. Is that true?"

I nodded. "I'm afraid so."

Charlotte lifted her veil. Her big dark eyes brimmed with tears.

Involuntarily, as if I had been pushed, I moved across the room to her.

She stepped into my arms. Her face was pressed against my chest, her long-legged body against mine. She sniffled back tears while I inhaled her sultry perfume and felt light-headed. She was the kind of woman who could make you feel half-dizzy.

After a few minutes she stopped crying and detached herself from my embrace with a cool but sexy look. She sat down in a client's chair next to my desk and took out a small pale handkerchief with which she dabbed at her eyes. I was a bit surprised that the handkerchief wasn't black, too.

I walked behind the desk and sat down in the swivel chair. I cleared my throat, assumed a professional manner. It felt false, but I waited for her to speak. When she didn't, I said, "How is your mother today?"

"Not well," Charlotte said. "Not well at all. She's taken to her bed. There is some suggestion of a stroke, but the doctor isn't really sure. Shirley's death was a terrible blow. Shirley was her favorite, as you probably had already figured out."

This was news to me. I had been under the impression that Shirley had been Hattie's *least* favorite.

"So how is the case progressing?" Charlotte asked.

"Slowly," I said.

"Have you discovered any new leads or clues, Michael?"

"Nothing worth mentioning," I said.

Charlotte snuck a peek at her watch, a thin strap of platinum and jewels. "I have to be at the theater in fifteen minutes. I need to talk to my director. Tonight's opening night, you know." She smiled. "I'm expecting you to be there, Michael."

"I don't have a ticket."

"Don't worry," she said. "I'll leave a *comp* for you at the box office. Front row center."

"You're not postponing anything, then?"

"Oh no," Charlotte said. "It's in the great tradition of the American stage to carry on no matter how tragic one's personal circumstances are. And besides, Shirley's funeral is not until Monday." She tapped her fingers along the edge of her purse. "Aren't you at all curious why I'm here?"

"This is not just a social visit?"

"Of course it's social," Charlotte said, "everything I do is social in one way or another, but I've got something to show you, too." She withdrew an envelope from her purse and handed it to me. "I found this among Shirley's private papers."

It was a document of sale transferring a 20 percent interest in Shirley Beaumont's shares in Ashtree Farm to Diane Carter.

"What do you make of it, Michael?"

"It looks like a simple bill of sale between your sister and Ms. Carter."

"It doesn't seem strange to you?"

"In what way strange?"

"What is Diane doing buying twenty percent of Shirley's shares? Where did she get the money? And why was Shirley selling them?"

"Did you ask her those questions?"

"Certainly not."

"Maybe there's a simple explanation. Maybe Shirley needed the money. Maybe Ms. Carter borrowed the money to buy the shares as an investment. Maybe the whole thing was a simple business transaction."

"Hah, I can see by that remark you don't know the Beaumont family very well. Beaumonts don't engage in simple business transactions. There's almost always some other explanation, some ulterior motive." Charlotte held her handkerchief to her nose. "In any case, I thought you might want to see it, perhaps investigate it a little further." Charlotte, frowning, added, "I have to admit that I'm somewhat disappointed that you don't see the significance of this document. It seems very strange and suspicious to me and certainly worth investigating."

I smiled at her. "Well, if you think it's worth investigating, I'll check it out."

Charlotte threw me a dazzling smile. "You're a dear." She stole another glance at her watch, stood up abruptly, and said, "Oh Lord, I have to run." She held out her gloved hand. "Don't see me out," she said. I stood up and reached across the desk and took hold of her hand. "Maybe we can have dinner together again really soon," she said. She looked invitingly at me. "Would you like that?"

Instead of nodding eagerly, I said, "Sure."

"Take care," Charlotte Beaumont said. She squeezed my fingers, turned, and swept grandly out of the room, as if she was making the third-act exit in her final appearance on the American stage. On her way out, she encountered McGraw, who appeared suddenly in the doorway, dressed in faded Levi's and a sweatshirt. An oversized St. Louis Cardinals baseball cap covered McGraw's head. With the comment, "My, but aren't you a cute little boy," Charlotte strode past McGraw and down the stairs.

McGraw said, "Downstairs, there are police and TV people all over the street. The window of the new restaurant is missing, and someone said somebody got shot at. You know anything about that?"

"A little bit," I said. "I'll tell you after you tell me about your day."

"Wait a minute," McGraw said. "Before I do that, I want to know who that person who just left the office was."

"Charlotte Beaumont."

"Yeah? Well, she can kiss my ass with her 'little boy' shit."

"Be cool," I said. "Go look at yourself in the mirror. You could pass for a thirteen-year-old paperboy."

"Oh yeah?"

"Take it easy," I suggested. "What are you so angry about anyway?"

"I'm pissed off," she said, "because I spent the morning in every orphanage in this part of Kentucky and couldn't find out a single thing. None of them ever heard of Eddie Walker."

"Where did you go?"

"I went to all three orphanages in Jefferson County. I went to the Shelby County Orphans' Home. I went to Saint John's Orphanage in Nelson County. The cover story about being an investigator with the State Bureau of Statistics worked beautifully. They didn't give me any trouble about looking at the records. It's just that there are no records on an Eddie Walker." She flopped angrily into the chair behind her desk. "What are we going to do now?"

I shrugged. "Punt, I guess." The phone on my desk rang. I grabbed up the receiver. "Rhineheart."

It was Diane Carter. "Mrs. Beaumont wants to see you, Michael. She's had a stroke and she's been confined to her bed, but she wants you there."

"I'll be there as soon as I can," I said. I put down the phone. "Hattie Beaumont wants to see me."

Preoccupied, McGraw nodded. "Is there any chance this orphanage information is wrong?"

I said, "Sure. It's all secondhand. Paige says Walker told her he grew up in an orphanage in the area." I frowned. "Wait a minute. 'This area' might include Southern Indiana, too. You been looking all over this side of the Ohio. What about the other side?"

"You mean New Albany? Jeffersonville?"

"Why not? They're right across the river. They're

both closer than some of the places you went to today." I picked up the phone and dialed Directory Assistance. "I want the number for Southern Indiana information." I handed the phone to McGraw and headed for the door. "You need me for anything I'll be out at Ashtree."

THIRTY-FOUR

It was 1:30 when I arrived at Ashtree. A pale, drawn Diane Carter met me at the door and showed me upstairs to Hattie's bedroom where a gray-haired nurse sat in a chair close to the bed. The bed was an antique four-poster that stood high off the floor. Hattie Beaumont was lying in it, a quilt covering her slight form. Her eyes were closed. She looked weak and old. There was an oxygen tank against the wall and next to it a hospital cart on rollers. The other side of the large room lay in shadow.

In a low voice, Diane said, "The doctor has given her a shot to help her sleep, but it won't take effect for a while. She hasn't spoken much... except to ask for you... If you need anything, I'll be in the library with Paige and Miss Hackett." She turned and left the room.

I approached the bed. Hattie Beaumont's eyes fluttered open. She looked at me blankly for a moment as if she didn't know me. Then, she made a slight gesture with her hand. I bent down over the bed.

Hattie's voice, when she spoke, was a reedy whisper: "Are... they... safe?"

"Who?"

"Where... are... they?"

"Who?"

"Paige."

"Downstairs, in the library."

"Diane."

"She's there, too."

"She's... there... too," she repeated the words back at me.

"Where," she said, "is... Charlotte?"

"I don't know."

"Are... they... *safe*?"

"Yeah," I said, "they're safe."

"Mr. Rhineheart... I want... you... to... I want ... to... hire you... again... I want you... to find ... Shirley's... murderer."

Hattie closed her eyes, as if the effort to speak a full sentence had worn her out completely. After a moment she opened them. "Will you... do that... for... me?"

I nodded. "I'll try," I said.

Hattie's lips moved—her voice was barely audible now. It sounded as if she had spoken the word *picture*. She gestured at the table next to her bed. I reached over and opened the table drawer. Inside was a standard-sized black-and-white photograph. It was a snapshot of four young children, two boys seated between two girls on a park bench. The boys looked to be about nine or ten years old, the girls several years younger. They were all fair-haired nice-looking children and they resembled each other in that they all wore glasses and none of them were smiling. They sat on the bench with their arms around each other peering stolidly at the camera. The girls both wore dresses with round collars and the boys were wearing slacks and open-necked dress shirts. In the background a group of trees and thick shrubbery was visible. On the white plastic border that framed the shot was the date Apr 64. Nothing about the picture, neither the children nor the setting seemed familiar or recognizable.

I held the picture in front of Hattie. "Is this what you wanted me to see?"

But the old woman's eyes had closed and the breath that issued from between her lips was shallow but even. I touched her forehead with my fingers. The skin was dry and hot. She didn't stir. I put the picture in my pocket.

The nurse stood up and came over to the bed. She took Hattie's pulse and said, "Mrs. Beaumont appears to have gone to sleep. Her pulse is fine. She seems to be all right, but I think she should be left alone for a while."

I thanked the woman and left the room. Downstairs, in the library Diane Carter was seated next to the tea cart. She held the cup in both hands as if she was afraid she would drop it. Meg Hackett was in a nearby chair, the ever-present sewing basket in her lap. Paige sat on the couch, a magazine in her lap. When I entered, Diane Carter stood up and said, "How is she?"

"Nurse says she's all right. She's sleeping," I said.

Meg Hackett spoke to me. "Mr. Rhineheart," she said, "your secretary, a Ms. McGraw just called. She left this number." She handed me a slip of paper, and indicated the phone on an end table near the couch.

"Thanks." I walked over and picked up the receiver and dialed the number. It was local long-distance with an Indiana area code. The phone was answered by a woman with a whispery voice who said, "Saint Dominic's."

I asked for McGraw and after a moment she came on the line. "You better get over here. There's someone you need to meet. She's got some heavy-duty information to lay on you." McGraw gave me the address and I hung up. I looked up to see everyone in the room staring at me.

"Will you have some tea, Mr. Rhineheart?" Diane Carter asked.

"No thanks," I said, "I don't have the time." I asked Diane Carter to keep me posted on Hattie Beaumont's condition, said goodbye to her and Paige and Miss Hackett and left the room. Paige got up and followed me. She caught up to me on the porch. I thought she was going to ask me about the photographs. Instead, she said, "I'm worried about Grandmother. Do you think she's going to be all right, Mr. Rhineheart?"

There was a strained, lost look on her face and the tone of her voice was that of a child who needed reassurance. I remembered what Hattie had said about her. Her father never visited her. Her mother had no time for her. It was hard to picture Charlotte Beaumont in the role of anyone's mother. Paige was young and rich and beautiful, but she hadn't been dealt much of a hand when it came to parents and family.

"She's going to be fine," I said, not at all sure that was true. "She's a tough woman."

The lost look vanished. Paige smiled. "She *is* tough. You're right."

"It's a valuable quality," I said. "Necessary even. I got to go, babe," I added, heading down the steps and across the drive to the car. As I was getting behind the wheel I looked back at the porch. Paige was still standing there. This time, instead of giving me the finger, she waved.

THIRTY-FIVE

SAINT Dominic's Orphanage Home was a squat redbrick building that reminded me of an old elementary school I attended as a kid. Infrequently. There was a high wire fence and a cement school yard with a hoop and a backboard. McGraw's VW was parked out front. McGraw was in the schoolyard playing basketball with a small dark-haired woman in jeans and a warm-up jacket. As I approached, the dark-haired woman dribbled toward the basket, swept past McGraw with a head fake, switched her dribble from her right hand to her left, and laid the ball in the basket.

McGraw took off her baseball cap and fanned herself. "Did you see that?" she asked me. "Is she something, or what?"

"Great," I said. "Can she dribble between her legs?"

"What's the matter with you?" McGraw said.

"What am I doing here, McGraw? You call me over to watch your friend shoot hoops?"

McGraw crossed her eyes and stuck out her tongue at me. Then she beckoned to the dark-haired woman, who tucked the ball under her arm and trotted over. The woman was an inch or two taller than McGraw and middle-aged with bright intelligent eyes. "Mary Agnes, I want to introduce you to Michael Rhineheart. Rhineheart, this is *Sister* Mary Agnes. She's director of Saint Dominic's."

I nodded hello. My first thought was that back when

I was in school all the nuns wore habits and veils. And they didn't have good schoolyard moves. My next thought was that I was beginning to remind myself of Farnsworth. Both thoughts made me feel old. "Nice lay-up, sister."

"Thank you, Mr. Rhineheart." Her voice was low-pitched, melodious. "Sally tells me that you are a private eye in the grand tradition."

A private-eye buff, I thought. I ran into them all the time. They weren't usually nuns though. "I don't know about grand or tradition," I said, "but I'm a private eye, all right."

"Your profession holds a good deal of fascination for me. You happen to be the first real life private eye I have ever encountered."

"I hear that often," I said. "Only it's not usually as well put."

"I'm a big mystery buff," Sister Mary Agnes said, "the classic British ones, thriller-dillers, hardboiled detective stuff. I like it all but I'm a particular fan of private eyes and private-eye writers. Lew Archer and Ross Macdonald. Marlow and Chandler. Spencer and Robert B. Parker. Do you ever read private-eye fiction, Mr. Rhineheart?"

"Once in a while," I said. "When I'm not on a case and I have the time."

The sister turned to Sally. "Is that Mr. Rhineheart's subtle way of reminding me he's here on business?"

"Could be," McGraw said, "but I'm not sure *subtle*'s the right word. He usually says what he means straight out."

I smiled at Sister Mary Agnes. "Have you been at Saint Dominic's long, sister?"

"Since 1959 when I was a novice. I was here when Eddie Walker came in 1963. I was one of his teachers. I taught him English and history. Eddie was not one of my prize pupils, but I remember him well. He was with us for ten years. From 1963 to 1973. When he left, he joined the navy, I believe." She handed me the basketball. "Would you mind holding this?" She reached into a pocket of her jacket and pulled out a ring of keys.

"Let's go inside where we can find a place to sit and be comfortable." She led us across the yard to a side door of the school, which she unlocked. We walked down a short flight of stairs and into a crowded little office that contained two filing cabinets, a desk, three chairs, a copier, a personal computer, a telephone, and a fax machine. Sister Mary Agnes sat down behind her desk. McGraw and I took chairs opposite.

I said, "When was the last time you saw Eddie, sister?"

"The day he left the home was the last time I saw him."

"Do you know anything about what happened to him after he left?"

Sister Mary Agnes shook her head. "I don't think I'm going to be able to be much help to you in that way. The only reason I'm talking to you at all is because I think you might be able to help him. My hope is that if he's done something wrong and you're looking for him maybe you can find him before the police do, maybe you can help him before it's too late."

"Maybe," I said.

"You sound rather doubtful," Sister Mary Agnes said.

"I don't know how much I can help Eddie. I'm fairly certain he took part in some bad..." I almost said *shit*, before I remembered where I was and who I was talking to. I substituted "...stuff. He's my only real lead. If I catch up with him I'm going to do what it takes to find out what he knows, and like McGraw says I'm not very subtle."

Sister Mary Agnes smiled. "You call Sally 'McGraw.' I think that's charming." She turned to McGraw. "It must be very liberating to be addressed by your last name. Like a man."

"I don't mind what he calls me," McGraw said, "just so long as he doesn't swear at me."

"Do you swear at Sally, Mr. Rhineheart?"

When it comes to swearing, I'm not even in McGraw's class, but I smiled at the nun and said, "Just once in a while, sister."

"I think you two are putting me on," she said, "but the truth is I don't mind. It's kind of fun." She gave me a steady look. "It's true, Mr. Rhineheart, you're not very subtle, but all in all you seem to be quite a dude, as one of my new students, whose name happens to be Jamal, would say. I'm a pretty good judge of character, I think, and I believe that it would be in Eddie's best interests to aid you in any way I can. Sally and I had a little talk before you arrived and I told her some things. She suggested that the best way I could be of help was to tell you about Eddie's closest friends."

I looked at McGraw. "I don't understand," I said. "His closest friends?"

"The Hacketts," McGraw said.

"The Hacketts?"

McGraw nodded. "Mary Margaret and Elizabeth and David and Thomas Hackett, Jr. The children of the man who was killed in the same accident that killed James Beaumont."

"The Hacketts were here at Saint Dominic's?"

"Oh yes."

"But Diane Carter told me she thought the Hacketts went to live with relatives."

"She was mistaken," Sister Mary Agnes said. "The Hacketts had no other living relatives."

"They were here at the same time that Eddie Walker was?"

Sister Mary Agnes nodded. "They arrived in the spring of 1964 and left sometime in the mid-seventies. While they were with us, the Hackett children and Eddie Walker were inseparable."

The Hackett children. The phrase made me reach

into my pocket and bring out the photograph from Hattie's desk. I handed it across the table to Sister Mary Agnes. "Why, yes," she said, nodding. "That's exactly how they looked when they first arrived. That's Thomas and that's David and the two girls"—she touched each image with her finger—"are Elizabeth and Mary Margaret." She handed the photo back to me. I put it in my pocket.

Mary Margaret. Meg. An image of the woman bent over her needlework came to me. "Do you know what happened to the Hacketts?"

Sister Mary Agnes shook her head. "They left us, of course, as all the children do, eventually. Some, a good many actually, are proud of their ties to the home and they keep in contact with us. We have a fairly active alumni association. Others, however, simply don't keep in touch. The Hacketts never did. The truth is I never expected them to. They were a rather strange family."

"What makes you say that?"

"I'm not sure, really. Outwardly, they were very ordinary children. Nice-looking. Fairly well behaved. But they kept to themselves and were very secretive and clannish. They made no friends with any of the other children. With the exception, that is, of Eddie. They took Eddie under their wing, and the truth is, I was never sure that was a good thing for Eddie. Even though Eddie needed friends.

"Psychologically, Eddie was a kind of scapegoat figure. The rest of the children picked on him. As a result, he acted out and was rather hostile. Eddie, I'm afraid, had the kind of personality that usually gets into trouble with the law. If you find him I do hope there's some way you can help him."

I nodded, trying to be sympathetic, but I was thinking about the fact that the case had suddenly leaped backward in time twenty-five years. It had taken on a new shape, a new reality. All of a sudden things that had appeared to be significant no longer seemed to matter.

The struggle to run Ashtree, for example. What did it have to do with the kidnapping? Maybe nothing.

Eddie Walker was connected to the family of the man who had died in what Diane had called "the Beaumont family's great tragedy." But it had been more than the Beaumonts' tragedy. It had been the Hacketts' tragedy as well. Four children orphaned. Moneyless, without a grandmother to take them in. What did that mean in terms of the case? Was the kidnapping something other than what it had appeared to be? Was that why the mare and the foal had not been returned? My mind was buzzing with a whole new set of questions that needed answers, and there wasn't enough time to figure them out. The Queen was due to arrive in Louisville the next day.

I thought about the phone conversation with Eddie. "They're loonies," he had said. "A crazy family." I looked at my watch. It had been hours since I had checked on Betty Walker. I asked Sister Mary Agnes if I could use her phone.

"Of course."

I dialed Midtown Investigations. Reardon himself answered and as soon as I heard his voice I knew that something had gone wrong.

"I been trying to get a hold of you. You're going to kick my ass on this one, Mickey."

"Your people didn't lose her, did they, John?"

"You got it, Mick. I don't know what to say. No excuse, of course. I can't tell you how sorry I am, buddy. It's my personnel's fault, but I'm taking full responsibility."

I stuffed down my anger. "Forget it," I said. "It happens."

"Let me bring you up to date as far as we had her and offer you whatever assistance you can use. Subject left her trailer at 12:35. She drove in her car to downtown Louisville. She parked her car at a parking meter near Third and Jefferson and entered the Miller Hotel.

THE QUEEN'S MARE

My operative parked down the block facing the same way. She was in the hotel approximately fifteen minutes and when she came out she got in her car and turned East on Liberty. She got on the North–South, took it to Eastern Parkway. My man stayed with her all the way. On the corner of Eastern Parkway and Preston, she turned right and pulled into the parking lot of a convenience store. She was in there 12 minutes, came out, got back in her car and headed West on Eastern Parkway. That's when my guy's car failed to start. He called in right away and I sent somebody out to the trailer park, but she hasn't shown up there yet. If she shows we'll call you right off. My trailer-park person's out there waiting and will stay until subject shows, and there's two or three other things we can do for you. I can send somebody to check the Miller and see who she visited, and if subject doesn't show at trailer park I got somebody who can do a quick black bag job on the trailer. As I said before, Mick, I can't tell you how sorry I am."

"John, I appreciate the offer. Let me think about it and get back to you." I hung up and stood there a moment lost in thought. Something was tugging at my memory. Eddie Walker had been calling from a phone booth on the corner of Fifth and Jefferson. Right down the block from the Miller Hotel.

McGraw poked me. "What's with the phone call? What's going on?"

I told her what had happened. "I want you to go back to the office and sit tight in case Farns or LT calls. When Farns calls tell him to come back to the office. If LT calls take down his information."

She nodded. "What about you? What are you going to do?"

"I'm going to pay a visit to the Miller Hotel."

Sister Mary Agnes said, "I hope I've been some help to you, Mr. Rhineheart."

"I appreciate what you've done, sister."

McGraw and Sister Mary Agnes exchanged hugs. Then the sister came over and threw her little arms around my waist. I was surprised—when I was a kid nuns weren't into hugging, they were into cracking my knuckles with a ruler—but managed to pat her clumsily on the back in return.

She said, "This case is important to you, isn't it?"

"I want to solve it, yeah."

"In that case, I'll say a prayer for your success," Sister Mary Agnes said.

I nodded. I needed all the help I could get on this one.

THIRTY-SIX

I took the Kennedy Bridge to downtown Louisville. I parked the Maverick in a DELIVERIES ONLY zone near the corner of Third and Jefferson and walked into the Miller lobby. The hotel had been built in the thirties and it looked as if it hadn't been cleaned since. The lobby was dingy and dimly lit, with seedy furniture and a thin, worn carpet. The desk clerk was short and fat with a dark mustache, a receding hairline, and a lisp.

"How can I help you, thir?"

I took out a twenty and laid it on the desk.

The clerk eyed the bill and smirked.

"Sandy-haired woman in her thirties was in here less than a hour ago. You remember her?"

"Yeth, indeed."

"Tell me about her visit."

The clerk tapped his fingers on the desk. He leered at the twenty.

I nodded.

The clerk's fingers tapped over and picked up the bill. "She visited Mithter Wilson in Six C. Was there about fifteen, twenty minutes."

"Mr. Wilson still in his room?"

The clerk shrugged. "I haven't seen him leave."

"What's Mr. Wilson look like?"

The clerk described Eddie Walker. He pointed to a corner of the lobby. "Elevators over there. But the stairs are quicker."

211

I took the stairs. I began to get winded between the third and fourth, and by the time I reached six, I had to stop for a few minutes and catch my breath. It was enough to make you wonder why you ran five miles four times a week. Six C was located in the middle of the corridor. I pressed my ear to the thin, scarred door. Nothing. No sound. I gave the door a rap with my knuckles. There was no response from inside.

I checked the lock. A hard look would have opened it. I used an expired credit card.

Inside, I shut the door quietly behind me and stood still for a moment taking in the place—a cramped rectangle of a room furnished in cheap, plastic hotel furniture: a double bed, two scarred end tables, a pair of mismatched lamps, a four-drawer dresser, a portable TV on a stand. At the rear of the room, next to the closet, a door to a bathroom stood partly open.

The open door caught my attention. As I stared at it I felt the muscles in my stomach begin to tense. I took out my Python and flipped off the safety. I began to cross the room slowly, noting things automatically. A copy of *Playboy* lay on one of the end tables. Next to it was a pack of Camel filters, and a ceramic ashtray half full of cigarette butts. On top of the chest of drawers there was a small radio, an alarm clock, and a green plastic air freshener device.

When I reached the partially open bathroom door, I gave it a little nudge. It swung forward less than six inches and stuck against something. Uh-oh. I took a deep breath, and peered around the door. Eddie Walker's body was lying on its back on the tile floor of the bathroom. He was fully clothed, denim shirt, jeans, boots. His pale gray eyes were wide open, fixed and sightless. Walker was dead, but the cause of his death was not immediately apparent. There was no blood, no visible wounds on his body. I knelt down next to the body and eased it on its side. At the base of the neck, barely visible, there was a small neat bullet hole surrounded by a half moon of caked blood. A .22. The weapon that Katz had called a woman's gun. I recalled Betty Walker's cold blue eyes. It looked as if she had dusted her ex-husband with one in the back of the neck, executioner-style. If so, what, besides one cold hard lady, did that make Betty? Not just somebody's wife, but a major player in the game.

I realized that I didn't really know anything about her, except that she had been married to Eddie Walker and had a retarded brother who lived in an East End institution. I thought about the man in a wheelchair, and it occurred to me that I had screwed up back at the rest home. I had forgotten to ask Dawn a basic question.

I went ahead and searched the body, finding keys and loose change and a couple of crumpled dollar bills in the front pockets. Walker's back pocket, where his wallet should have been, was empty.

I got to my feet, and found myself facing my own reflection in the mirrored front of the medicine cabinet. I had a gun in my hand and a grim, bleak look on my face, which was pale and unshaven and red-eyed. I looked mean and nasty, like somebody a pack of dogs ought to chase. I put away my weapon and ran my hand across my face, as if I could wipe away the feeling the sight of Walker's dead body had produced. Sister Mary Agnes had called him a scapegoat, someone who took the blame for others' sins and crimes. He was beyond blame now, a body lying on the cold floor of a bathroom in a cheap hotel. If he had died for someone's sins, it didn't make his death any prettier or him any less dead.

The place needed to be searched, but I really didn't have the time for anything except a cursory walk-through. I looked under the bed, ran my hands down the back of the couch, opened the dresser and rummaged through the drawers. It took me all of ten minutes and when I was finished the only thing I found that mattered was an envelope in the pocket of Eddie's jean jacket. The envelope contained the photographs that Paige had wanted me to look for.

I stuck the envelope into my pocket and went into the bathroom, where I grabbed a towel off the rack and wiped down everything I had touched. I wasn't quite sure why I was doing this. Habit, I supposed. Once the body was found the desk clerk would describe me to the police and Katz would know exactly who the visitor to Walker's room had been. As I left the room, I pulled the door closed behind me, locking it. I took the stairs down to the lobby, which was deserted. The clerk was probably hiding somewhere.

Out front, there was a ticket on my car. I snatched it off the window and threw it in the gutter. I got in and started it up and drove to a package liquor store on the corner of Fifth and Muhammud Ali. I bought a half pint of bourbon, drank it in three swallows. Then I used the pay phone to call the office. McGraw answered.

"LT just called," she said. "He gave me the names of thirty-five red Toyota pickup owners in the surrounding counties. One of them is Thomas Hackett, Jr., who lives at Number 9 Old Farm Road in Shelbyville."

A farm. Of course. That was where Winterset was. "Eddie Walker is dead," I said. "His ex-wife killed him."

McGraw didn't say anything. Her silence was all right with me. When you thought about it what was there to say?

"Is Farns there?" I asked.

"Farns is here," she said. "I filled him in. We'll be ready to go as soon as you get here."

"I'll be there in a little while," I said. "I just got to make a call."

"Where are we going first?" McGraw asked. "Ashtree or Hackett's farm?"

"We're going out to Hackett's and get the mare and the foal. And the money."

THE QUEEN'S MARE

I hung up, then threw a quarter in the phone and dialed Saint Dominic's. I was put through to Sister Mary Agnes's office.

"Sister, it's Michael Rhineheart."

"What can I help you with, Michael?"

"I want to ask you about the other Hackett brother. David."

"What about him?"

"Was he retarded?"

"How did you know that, Michael?"

"I'm a private eye, sister."

THIRTY-SEVEN

We took one car and three guns. The Maverick and my Python, along with the snub-nosed .32 I had strapped to my ankle, plus Farnsworth's .38 police special, which he always carried in a holster at the back of his belt. McGraw sat up front, Farns in the back. On the way we tried to sort it all out, decide who was who, and figure out the motive. Betty Walker was Elizabeth. Thomas Jr. the driver of the red pickup. Meg, of course, was Mary Margaret and had been their inside person. The identity part was easy, the motive was the problem.

Farnsworth thought it was simple revenge.

"Revenge for *what*?" I asked.

"Revenge on the Beaumonts because Hattie's son was responsible for the death of Thomas Hackett, Sr., and his wife—their mother and father."

"You mean you think they hatched some kind of plot and have been keeping it alive for twenty-five years?"

"Stranger things have happened," Farnsworth said.

"The whole thing was just an accident," McGraw said. "Why would they want to get even for an accident?"

Farnsworth shrugged. "Maybe they don't see it that way."

The discussion petered out and we drove the rest of the way in silence, each of us keeping our thoughts to ourselves. On the outskirts of Shelbyville, I pulled over on a broad strip of grass that separated a flimsy-looking wire fence from Highway 26, a narrow two-lane side road that ran east and west across Shelby County.

The other side of the fence was the farm that belonged to Thomas Hackett, Jr. Clumps of trees. A field of tall grass and wild flowers that ran for several hundred yards back to a large weatherbeaten farmhouse. The red Toyota pickup and Betty's yellow Chevette were parked in a gravel drive alongside the house. Behind the house was a group of outbuildings: a shed, a small barn, and a silo. Beyond the outbuildings was a line of thick woods.

McGraw handed me the binoculars. I trained them first on the farmhouse and then on the other structures and then swept them across the rest of the property. Except for the vehicles the place looked deserted—the house and the buildings ramshackle, unpainted.

"What do you see, kid?" Farnsworth asked from the backseat.

"Nothing."

"What do we do now?" McGraw said.

"Go get something to eat," I said. "We'll come back when it's dark."

"You think the mare's in the barn?" Farnsworth asked.

"I don't know, Farns. I hope so."

I made a U-turn and drove into Shelbyville. McGraw wanted to eat at Science Hill, a restaurant on Washington Street that was known for its good food, but it was closed. We settled on some Kentucky Fried, which we ate with plastic forks on a vinyl table inside a boxy harshly lighted over–air-conditioned restaurant. Farnsworth and McGraw got into an argument about crispy versus original recipe, but I wasn't listening. I was thinking about the layout of the Hackett place and the best way to approach the barn and the farmhouse.

We had dessert, some kind of jellied cake that McGraw made a face at and wouldn't touch, and lingered at the restaurant until nearly eight o'clock. It was getting dark quickly and the temperature was falling when we drove back to Highway 26. I parked in the same spot.

We sat quietly for ten minutes and waited for it to be completely dark. The house remained unlighted, a large, shadowy silhouette. I could see the outlines of the two vehicles in the drive. I took one last look at my watch: 8:12. Charlotte Beaumont was getting ready to go on stage. In my own way so was I. I flipped off the interior light and we got out of the Maverick.

"I'm going to need you to stay up here," I told McGraw.

"What for?" McGraw said.

"I need backup, babe. Someone to stay with the car, watch our butts."

"Backup, huh? Sounds like another half-ass assignment to me, a woman's job. I want to go in with you two."

"Backup's no half-ass thing. It's an important job."

"Why can't I go in?"

"For one thing, we need you here. For another, you're not packing a piece, which gives us that much less firepower in case we need it."

"Who says I'm not packing." She whipped a wicked-looking little Beretta out of her purse. We had, it seemed, four guns.

"I still need you here," I said.

McGraw muttered to herself, but nodded.

I said to Farnsworth, "You got your flashlight with you tonight, old man?"

"Left-hand coat pocket."

I stepped over and pressed down on the top strand of wire. Already sagging, the fence folded up. Farnsworth stepped over the jumble of wire onto the farm property. I followed. We walked slowly down through the field, using the trees as cover, circled around behind the house, and headed for the barn. The night sky was clear. A sliver of moon hung above the line of woods.

We heard nothing, saw no one. The place seemed to be deserted.

We passed the shed and approached the barn. I peered through the structure's single window. It was too dark to see inside. I unlatched the barn door and stepped inside. Farnsworth was right behind me. It was too dark to see anything at first, but from somewhere in the barn I heard a rustle of hay, a stirring. I sensed the presence of something or someone.

I was about to tell Farnsworth to use the flashlight when I heard it click on and saw, a half dozen feet in front of me, the mare, Winterset, and her foal, caught suddenly, encircled, in the flashlight's beam.

The flashlight clicked off abruptly and I was left with a quick freeze-frame impression of a magnificent-looking animal, a well-set head, held erect, eyes flashing in the sudden light, a long neck and a full dark mane, powerful shoulders, and smooth burnished flanks. And next to it a spindly-legged ten-day-old foal so small it almost looked like a different species of animal.

"Jesus," Farnsworth's voice in the darkness sounded solemn and awestruck.

"Hold off on the flashlight," I said. "We don't want to show any more light than we have to. Our eyes'll adjust in a minute."

"That's them," Farnsworth said. "Winterset and the foal. Not much question."

"You know anything about horses, old man?" I asked. "I'm not talking about handicapping them. I'm talking about feeding them and shit like that. What I mean is, can you tell if they're okay or not?"

"I just saw them that second," Farnsworth said, "but they looked okay to me."

Gradually, I was able to make out the outlines of the mare and the foal. I put my gun in its holster and walked over close to the mare, who shifted her feet slightly. "You think it's okay if I pet her?" I asked Farnsworth.

"I don't see why not," Farnsworth said. "Careful

though. She's an awful expensive animal."

I reached out and patted her flank and as I did I heard the barn door swing open behind us. The sound raised the hairs on the back of my neck. As an overhead light came on, I swung around to see Betty Walker and a medium-sized man wearing thick glasses standing in the doorway. Betty had a gun—a .22—in her left hand. Her right was on the light switch fastened to the wall next to the door. The man wearing the glasses was the pickup driver who had tried to take me off with a shotgun earlier that day. He was holding the shotgun now with both hands and he looked relaxed, as if he was familiar and comfortable with the weapon.

Betty's weapon was trained on Farnsworth. The shotgun was pointed directly at me. It was a double-barreled Ithaca capable of blowing out the side of a barn. Literally.

The man smiled at me. "You dumb sonofabitch," he said. "You wouldn't let it alone, would you?"

"Your name must be Hackett," I said.

"That's right. Tom Hackett Junior. My daddy was the man who was killed by James Beaumont. That drunken sonofabitch also killed my mother and orphaned me and my sisters. We grew up without any mother and father, but we're doing all right. We've been taking care of each other and we're still a family and we intend to get us some justice off the family of the man who murdered our parents."

"What are we talking about here?" I said. "I heard it was an automobile accident."

"You call it what you want to, mister. We Hacketts know what it was. James Beaumont was drunk and he drove that car into an approaching truck. He might just as well have taken a gun and shot them. Dead is dead. And orphans are orphans. My daddy was a moral man. He believed in justice. He used to tell us kids, an eye for an eye, a tooth for a tooth. Do what you have to do, is another thing he told us. And that's what we're doing"—he made a gesture to include his sister—"what we have to do."

"Vengeance?"

Hackett shook his head angrily. "Not vengeance. Not vengeance at all. What we're doing is meting out justice. Retribution. Righting a wrong."

"Looks like vengeance to me," I said. Maybe if I could keep him talking long enough... I'd think of something to do. Or Farns might come up with something. Or McGraw might see the light in the barn and come investigating. As long as Hackett was talking or listening, he wasn't shooting. "The whole thing happened twenty-five years ago. You're taking revenge on innocent people who weren't even responsible for what occurred."

"That's not true," Betty Walker said.

"What did Shirley Beaumont have to do with what her father did twenty-five years ago?"

"She's his daughter. She's a Beaumont," Hackett said, "the same as him."

"You kill your husband, Eddie," I said to Betty. "Why?"

Betty's face was pale but hard. "He was going to turn us in. He was... a weak man."

"You kill somebody because they're weak? That doesn't sound like justice to me."

Hackett's voice cut like a whip across the barn: "You don't know what the fuck you're talking about." His face was mottled with rage. "You're just a nosy fuckass private eye who's got no real stake in this matter. And you're going to die for your interest, friend. You and your partner. You're going to die along with all the Beaumonts and anyone else who gets in our way."

"What are you going to do after you've killed everyone? Go and live happily ever after on the million dollars you stole?"

"The money doesn't mean anything to us," Hackett said scornfully. "You don't think we're doing this for the money, do you? The goddamn money is sitting in the same suitcase in the hall closet and you can go count it yourself. Not a cent of it's been touched. Hell, we might burn it for all I know. After we dispense some justice. We don't give a shit about your employer's money, friend."

"What are you going to do with the mare and the foal?"

"None of your business," Betty Walker said.

"Tell him," Hackett said.

"It's none of his business," she said.

"Go ahead and tell him. We're going to kill him anyway, so it doesn't make any difference."

Betty said, "We're going to put it to death. Painlessly. It and the foal. That'll be the final act of justice," she said proudly.

"Painlessly," I repeated. "You two are some fucking pair," I said.

"What about Mary Margaret?" Farnsworth said. "What part is she playing in all this?"

Hackett swung the shotgun toward Farnsworth and smiled. "Meg has the best job of all," he said. "She's going to kill the old woman." He swung the gun back on me. "Friend, you got about thirty seconds left to live."

I looked over at Farnsworth. "Old man," I said, and winked at him, "I guess this is as good a day to die as any." It was a line from an old movie and my cue for us to make some kind of move—go for our guns, rush them, try something, but before we had a chance to make a move, McGraw's voice came galloping into the room.

"You two Hacketts drop your weapons, or I'll blow a hole in the back of both your heads."

The Hacketts froze but kept their weapons pointed at us. A Mexican standoff, of sorts. There was a momentary silence then McGraw's voice boomed out, "This is Detective Sergeant McGraw of the Kentucky

State Police. The place is surrounded. Drop your weapons and surrender." It sounded as if McGraw was speaking from just outside the door.

Betty Walker turned to her brother. "Oh God, Tom, what are we going to do?" The .22 hung loosely in her hand.

"We got hostages," Hackett said loudly. "You make a move on us and we'll kill them." He beckoned to me. "Get over here."

I shook my head.

"Come over here, or I'll kill you where you stand." He raised his weapon, aimed, and screamed in pain as a bullet from McGraw's Beretta slammed into his elbow, shattering it. The shotgun was jerked out of his hands by the impact. It skittered across the ground, and Hackett sank to his knees, clutching his arm and what was left of his elbow. Blood began to stream down his arm. Betty let the weapon fall out of her fingers and knelt next to her brother.

Farnsworth walked over and picked up her .22. He looked at me and shook his head in admiration. "That girlie. She something or what?"

McGraw jumped into the room like a commando, and crouched over Hackett, the Beretta pointed at his face, her left hand gripping her right wrist. Like the rest of us, she had seen too many movies, watched too much TV. Hackett had passed out from the pain.

Betty looked up at her. "You shot him."

McGraw nodded. Her lips were drawn back over her teeth and she was breathing hard. She said, "You're goddamn right I shot him. Did you think I was fucking around?"

"You can ease up now, babe," I said.

She nodded and stood up out of her crouch.

"That was a hell of a move," I said.

She nodded again.

"You saved our ass."

Farnsworth nodded. "You done good."

"Well," McGraw said. "I done well."

Farnsworth shrugged. "Have it your own way."

She blinked and looked around the room.

"Tomorrow, or one of these days," I said, "if you want, we'll go down together and put in for your investigator's license. It looks like it's about time."

"Sounds good," she said. Then she looked down at Hackett's bloody arm, gulped, and turned pale. Beads of sweat popped out on her forehead. She turned her head and threw up on the ground. It was over with quickly. She got a Kleenex out of her purse and wiped her mouth. She put the Kleenex and the Beretta in her purse, and said, "Hadn't we better see about his arm?"

Hackett's arm was in bad shape, but the bleeding eased up almost immediately. Farnsworth and I took him and Betty up to the farmhouse. McGraw volunteered to stay in the barn with Winterset and her foal. The suitcase with the money was in the hall closet exactly where Hackett said it would be. We put the Hacketts on the front couch and while Farnsworth kept them covered, I called Katz.

"Got a deal for you, Sergeant."

"What kind of deal?"

"Your end you get a dead body, the killer, and Shirley Beaumont's murderer. That's two collars on two different killers, plus a famous broodmare, a foal, and a million-dollar ransom."

It was quiet for a full minute and then Katz said, "What's your end?"

"My end," I said, "is no publicity on the mare and the foal and the ransom. You return these items to the proper owner on the sly. No media involvement."

"I can't promise shit like that."

"It's been nice talking to you," I said.

"Don't hang up," Katz said quickly. "I'll see what I can do."

I told him where to find Eddie Walker's body.

THE QUEEN'S MARE

"Who offed him?"

"His wife."

"Nice."

"We—me and Farnsworth—are holding her and her brother out here. He's the one who killed Shirley Beaumont. He's wounded and needs medical attention. And McGraw is out in the barn watching the broodmare and her foal. You better bring along a veterinarian too."

"Sounds like you got some kind of fucking circus out there. Gimme some directions."

I told him how to get to the farm.

"I'll be there in twenty-five minutes tops, and the first thing I want to see when I come in the door is your face. We got a lot of ground to cover."

"Sorry about that," I said. "I'm not going to be available when you get out here. Farnsworth'll brief you. I got to go tie up a few things."

"Wait a—"

I put down the phone. I indicated the Hacketts. "I guess I don't have to tell you to be careful with those two," I said to Farnsworth as I headed for the door.

"Not to worry," Farnsworth said. "You going out to Ashtree?"

I nodded.

"Hope it's not too late."

"Me too," I said, but in most of the ways that mattered it was already too late. It was too late for Shirley Beaumont and Eddie Walker and too late for the Hackett family. It had been too late a long time ago.

THIRTY-EIGHT

The gate guard at Ashtree wanted to telephone the main house to see if I was expected.

He was a black guy in his mid-thirties with a mustache. His uniform was neat and well-pressed and official-looking. He was leaning against my window.

"I don't want you to do that," I said.

"Those are my orders," he said.

I took out my weapon and stuck it in his face. "I don't have time to fuck with you." I opened the door. "Get in and drive me up to the house," I said. I kept the gun on him as I slid over in the seat.

"Mister, I think you're making a big mistake," the guard said, getting behind the wheel.

"Shut up and drive," I said. I kept the gun on him all the way to the house. When we pulled up in front of the porch, I reached over and took the Smith & Wesson out of his holster. "I'll return this to you later. Right now, I don't want you in my way. I want you to get out of the car and walk back to the entrance. When you get there, do whatever you want to, call the police ...whatever."

"Like I said, I think you're making a mistake, mister."

I cocked the weapon. "Get out of the car and start walking."

The guard opened the door, climbed out, and began walking briskly back down the road. I got out of the

Maverick and walked up the steps onto the porch, wondering why it was that no matter where a case took you, somehow at the end you always came back to where you started. And like the poet said, you knew the place for the first time.

I tried the door, but it was locked. I punched the bell, and after a minute the door swung open. Paige stood there, looking about the same as she had looked five days ago when I first rang the bell.

"Mr. Rhineheart," she said in a surprised voice.

"Hello, Paige."

She pointed to the Smith & Wesson I was holding. "You're carrying a gun. How come you're carrying a gun?"

"It's not mine," I said. I stuck it in my belt. "I'm just holding it for someone." I stepped into the hall. I stuck my hand in my pocket and took out the envelope I'd found in Eddie Walker's jean jacket. "Here, you better burn these."

"Oh God, thanks."

"Who's here, Paige?"

"You mean now? In the house?"

"Yeah."

"Diane and Mr. Glass and Mrs. Morehead, the cook, and Miss Hackett and Grandmother."

"Who's Mr. Glass?"

"He's the farm manager."

"What about the nurse? Where is she?"

"Miss Hackett gave her the night off."

"Tell me exactly where everyone is."

"Diane and Mr. Glass are in the library. Mrs. Morehead is in the kitchen, I think, and Miss Hackett is up in Grandmother's room with Grandmother."

"She been up there long?"

"About a half hour." Paige frowned. "It's kind of strange, really."

"What's strange?"

"Miss Hackett has Grandmother's door locked. I

went up to see her a few minutes ago and she wouldn't let me in. She said she didn't want to disturb Grandmother. She said I could see her tomorrow."

I nodded. "Tell me something," I said. "Besides the door at the top of the stairs, are there any other ways to get into your grandmother's room?"

"There's the guest bedroom."

"Where's that?"

"It's the room next to Grandmother's. There's an adjoining door."

"One more thing." I pointed at the stairway. "Is that the only way upstairs?"

Paige shook her head. "There's a back stairs."

"Show me," I said.

"Okay." I followed her through several downstairs rooms into the kitchen, where a large woman wearing an apron sat at a table making entries in a ledger. "This is Mrs. Morehead," Paige said, as we walked past her. "Mrs. Morehead, this is Mr. Rhineheart."

"'Lo," she said.

"Nice to meet you," I said.

Mrs. Morehead looked at the Smith & Wesson tucked in my belt, then looked quickly away.

I followed Paige into the back hall.

"There." She pointed to a narrow set of stairs. "What's going on, Mr. Rhineheart?"

"I'm tying up some loose ends, babe."

"Is anything wrong?"

"Nothing that can't be fixed," I said.

"Is there anything I can do to help?"

I nodded. "Yeah. Where's your room?"

"In the west wing." She pointed to her right.

"Downstairs?"

"Yes."

"You can help me out a lot by going straight to your room and locking yourself in and not coming out until I come and knock on your door."

"You want me to do that now?"

"Right now."

"Should I be scared, or something?"

"You trust me?"

"Yes."

"Do I look scared?"

"No."

"If I'm not scared, then there's nothing to be scared of. Now go ahead to your room. Lock yourself in and wait for me to come."

"Whatever you say." Paige turned and left the hall.

I took out the Smith & Wesson and checked the chamber. It was not my gun, but it would do. A gun was a gun. I hoped I wouldn't have to use it.

I went up the stairs slowly and quietly. The second-floor hallway was lined with antique pieces and lit by dim wall sconces. The carpet was thick, muffling my footsteps as I moved down the hall toward the guest room door. When I reached it, I opened it quietly, stepped inside, and closed the door behind me.

The guest bedroom was smaller than Hattie's room. A large queen-sized bed took up most of the space. There was a dressing table with a mirror on one side of the bed. A pair of chairs, a couch, and an end table on the other side. The door to Hattie's room was behind the couch. It was closed and locked on this side with a simple chain-lock device. I crossed the room carefully. I stood with my ear pressed to the wood, trying to hear something, but the door was too thick. I knelt down and put my eye to the keyhole. All I could see was part of a wall, a section of a window frame, the edge of a drape.

I stood up. I took a deep breath and looked at the chain-lock, thinking that what I needed right now was someone to say a prayer that it wasn't locked on the other side. It was too bad I didn't have Sister Mary Agnes along, or even LT's mother. I could have used either or both of them. I had forgotten any prayers I knew and I doubted if anyone would listen to mine, but just to be safe I muttered, "Please, let it be open," under my breath and slid the chain back quietly. I put my hand on the knob and turned and pulled the door. It came open slowly. With my right hand I took the Smith & Wesson out of my belt and stepped through the doorway.

Neither of the two people in the room noticed me. Not Hattie, who was lying in her bed, her head propped up by pillows. Nor Mary Margaret Hackett who was seated in the nurse's chair at the side of the bed, facing Hattie. Hattie's eyes were fixed on Meg Hackett, whose back was to me, and who was talking rapidly and steadily in a tight, choked voice that trembled with an undercurrent of rage you could hear from the other side of the room.

"What I'm talking about," she was saying, "is justice and retribution. Justice for Thomas Hackett and his family. Punishment for the Beaumonts. It was your son's willful act that destroyed a family. It was your drunken sot of a son who killed a loving mother and father and sent four young children to live as orphans. It's all documented. My brother put it all down in the journal we kept at the orphanage. It's there written down for everyone to see. It was James Beaumont's doing, and that's why we killed his daughter. And that's why we're going to kill all the Beaumonts.

"For you see," she went on, her voice beginning to rise and fall in a deranged singsong cadence that held Hattie transfixed and kept me rooted to the spot in the doorway, "the blood flows down to the children, and all those who bear the Beaumont name and share Beaumont blood are guilty. And will pay. With their money. And their property. And their precious possessions. But above all with their lives." She nodded at this and said, "Oh yes, oh yes."

In a voice that was weak but distinct, Hattie Beaumont spoke: "You poor thing...you're sick, aren't you?" Her eyes never left Meg Hackett's face.

Meg Hackett rose up out of her chair. The sewing basket that usually sat on her lap spilled to the floor. She was holding a pair of sewing scissors, which she pointed at Hattie. "How dare you call me a poor thing ... you dirty old ... *bitch* ... you ... evil old—"

It was, I figured, time to make a move. "That's enough, Mary Margaret," I said, loud enough to make her spin around and face me. She looked startled.

"You," she hissed. "How did you—"

"Listen to me," I said. "I've been out to the farm. I found the mare and the foal and the money. Your brother and sister are under arrest. The whole thing's over now. It's time to stop all this shit."

She laughed, a harsh mirthless sound. "Yes," she said, "sure, that's what someone like you would say. You are a ... a hired gun. You have no stake in the matter. Where is your family? Has your family been destroyed by someone's drunken act? What happened to your brothers and sisters? Did they go to orphans' homes? Don't tell me the whole thing's over. Don't tell me to stop." She gripped the scissors in her hand and held it up for me to see. "You see these? They are going to serve as my instrument of retribution."

I brought the Smith & Wesson up and leveled it at her chest.

"Mr. Rhineheart." An imploring look on her face, Hattie Beaumont stared across the room at me. "Don't shoot her. Please. She's sick. She's—"

Meg made a sound that was halfway between a shriek and a groan, wheeled about, and raised the scissors above her head with both hands. Before I squeezed the trigger, the last thing I saw was Hattie staring up at the scissors about to descend. The shot caught Mary Margaret in the back of the head, blowing away half of her brain, and killing her instantly. Her body pitched forward across the foot of the bed, coming to rest at Hattie Beaumont's feet.

I didn't run across the room to see to Hattie. The

fact is I stumbled over to a chair and sat down. I was still holding the gun. I wanted to put it down somewhere, but I couldn't unlock my grip on it. It was as if my fingers wouldn't work properly. I sat there for a long time. I tried not to think about what had just happened and what I had just done. Thinking about it made me feel tired. Infinitely tired. I wasn't sure I would ever be able to get up out of the chair. Or want to.

Finally, when I felt I could stand up, I got up and walked over to the bed. I was going to say something, something stupid like *It's going to be all right, Mrs. Beaumont*. But when I looked down at her, I could see that the life had gone out of her small, frail body and that her eyes were open and fixed, staring at nothing.

THIRTY-NINE

I was sitting between McGraw and Farnsworth on a barstool at O'Brien's, watching the Queen's arrival in Louisville on the big color TV. She was descending a set of iron steps to the runway. In the background stood a Royal Air Force jet. She wore a polka-dot dress and a funny little hat.

"She's not a real snappy dresser," McGraw said.

"With her money," Farnsworth said, "what does she care?" He took a sip of beer.

A television commentator's voice was talking about the royal visitor's plans to spend two days in the Commonwealth and to visit her famous broodmare and her new foal, which were stabled at, the commentator said, "the fabulous and world-famous Ashtree Farms, just outside of Louisville, which has been the subject of recent publicity owing to the untimely and unfortunate death of one of the racing industry's brightest personalities, the Matriarch of Ashtree, Hattie Beaumont."

At the bottom of the steps, a young girl in a dress stepped forward, curtsied, and handed the Queen a large bouquet of pink and yellow flowers.

"She's not supposed to do that," McGraw said.

"Do what?" Farnsworth asked.

"Curtsy. Americans don't curtsy."

"God, you're critical," Farnsworth said.

"Well, they don't," McGraw said. "We don't curtsy to anyone. It's the principle of the thing."

"I bet if you was out there at the airport," Farnsworth said, "you'd do a little knee-bending like everyone else."

McGraw shook her head. "I don't think so."

I took a drink of my beer. It was Sunday and legally all you could drink was beer.

The Queen began to walk along a line of local politicians. A tall bald man in a business suit bowed and took her hand.

"Look at that," Farnsworth said. He turned to McGraw. "Men don't curtsy. They bow." His tone was informative.

McGraw rolled her eyes up at the ceiling. "Big fucking news."

The Queen's consort appeared behind her.

Farnsworth pointed him out. "There's her husband. He always walks behind her. That's because he's not king. He's what you call a consort."

McGraw said, "I don't know what we'd do if we didn't have you to enlighten us on all these facts, old man."

Farnsworth shrugged. "Just sit around and be ignorant, I guess."

"He's still a good-looking man," McGraw said, her eyes on the Prince Consort's figure. "Very romantic and dashing. You don't see a lot of dashing anymore."

Farnsworth looked down the bar at a tattooed youth who was chug-a-lugging a mug. "Especially around here," he said.

The television announcer began to talk about what he called the Queen's famous love for horses. It was widely known, he said, that she felt that her horses were a part of her family and that they deserved a good deal of time, attention, and consideration.

McGraw turned to me. "You're not usually this quiet. How come? You thinking about the old lady?"

"Yeah," I said. But I wasn't. I was thinking about the Hacketts and the Beaumonts, about families and the things they did to each other and to others. I was thinking about the scene in Hattie's bedroom. I was remembering the things that Meg Hackett had said. Where's your family? she had asked me. I didn't answer her, but if I had I wondered what I would have said. Where *was* my family? My original family, my mother and father, were dead. My wife Catherine was dead. I had no children, no brothers or sisters. Did that mean that I didn't have a family? Or was your family where you found it? Not necessarily blood, but people for whom you felt some kind of kinship. If that was so, then it looked as if McGraw and Farnsworth were what I had for family. An old pro and a frizzy-haired secretary who wanted to be a private eye. They weren't much, but they were mine. And vice versa.

Wanda Jean came down the bar. She was tending bar this night.

"You know what the troubles with Sundays are?" she asked.

"You can't buy whiskey?" I said.

She shook her head. "Un-uh. It's that they're so long. I guess," she added, "that they're not really any longer than the other days. It just seems that way."

"I'm buying this round," I said. "What do you all want?"

"All you can get is beer," McGraw said. "Buying's no big deal when all you can drink is beer. You can't order something exotic and expensive like a triple strawberry daiquiri."

"We don't have those anyway," Wanda Jean said.

"You don't have to drink beer," Farnsworth said. "You could have a Coke."

"I'll take another beer," McGraw said.

"I thought it was my turn to buy," Farnsworth said.

"Give them whatever they want," I told Wanda Jean, "and give yourself one, too." I took out some money and laid it on the bar.

IF IT'S MURDER, CAN DETECTIVE J.P. BEAUMONT BE FAR BEHIND?...

FOLLOW IN HIS FOOTSTEPS WITH FAST-PACED MYSTERIES BY J.A. JANCE

TRIAL BY FURY　　　　75138-0/$3.95 US/$4.95 CAN

IMPROBABLE CAUSE　　75412-6/$3.95 US/$4.95 CAN

INJUSTICE FOR ALL　　89641-9/$3.95 US/$4.95 CAN

TAKING THE FIFTH　　　75139-9/$3.95 US/$4.95 CAN

UNTIL PROVEN GUILTY　89638-9/$3.95 US/$4.95 CAN

A MORE PERFECT UNION
　　　　　　　　　　　　75413-4/$3.95 US/$4.95 CAN

DISMISSED WITH PREJUDICE
　　　　　　　　　　　　75547-5/$3.50 US/$4.25 CAN

MINOR IN POSSESSION
　　　　　　　　　　　　75546-7/$3.95 US/$4.95 CAN

Buy these books at your local bookstore or use this coupon for ordering:

Avon Books, Dept BP, Box 767, Rte 2, Dresden, TN 38225
Please send me the book(s) I have checked above. I am enclosing $_____
(please add $1.00 to cover postage and handling for each book ordered to a maximum of three dollars). Send check or money order—no cash or C.O.D.'s please. Prices and numbers are subject to change without notice. Please allow six to eight weeks for delivery.

Name _____

Address _____

City _____ State/Zip _____

Jance 4/90